THE MAN FROM BATTLE FLAT

**Center Point
Large Print**

**This Large Print Book carries the
Seal of Approval of N.A.V.H.**

THE MAN FROM BATTLE FLAT

A Western Trio

LOUIS L'AMOUR

Edited by Jon Tuska

CENTER POINT PUBLISHING
THORNDIKE, MAINE

This Circle Ⓥ Western is published by
Center Point Large Print in 2010 in co-operation with
Golden West Literary Agency.

The text of this Large Print edition is unabridged.
In other aspects, this book may vary
from the original edition.
Printed in the United States of America
on permanent paper.
Set in 16-point Times New Roman type.

ISBN: 978-1-60285-749-0

Library of Congress Cataloging-in-Publication Data

L'Amour, Louis, 1908–1988.
   The man from Battle Flat : a western trio / Louis L'Amour ;
   edited by Jon Tuska. — 1st ed.
      p. cm. — (A Circle V western)
   ISBN 978-1-60285-749-0 (lib. bdg. : alk. paper)
   1. Large type books. I. Tuska, Jon. II. Title. III. Series.
   PS3523.A446M323 2010
   813′.52—dc22

                                                        2009048864

TABLE OF CONTENTS

Foreword   7

Mistakes Can Kill You   13

The Rider of the Ruby Hills   31

The Man from Battle Flat   215

FOREWORD

by Jon Tuska

Louis Dearborn LaMoore (1908-1988) was born in Jamestown, North Dakota. He left home at fifteen and subsequently held a wide variety of jobs although he worked mostly as a merchant seaman. From his earliest youth, L'Amour had a love of verse. His first published work was a poem, "The Chap Worth While," appearing when he was eighteen years old in his former hometown's newspaper, the *Jamestown Sun*. It is the only poem from his early years that he left out of SMOKE FROM THIS ALTAR which appeared in 1939 from Lusk Publishers in Oklahoma City, a book which L'Amour published himself; however, this poem is reproduced in THE LOUIS L'AMOUR COMPANION (Andrews and McMeel, 1992) edited by Robert Weinberg. L'Amour wrote poems and articles for a number of small circulation arts magazines all through the early 1930s and, after hundreds of rejection slips, finally had his first story accepted, "Anything for a Pal" in *True Gang Life* (10/35). He returned in 1938 to live with his family where they had settled in Choctaw, Oklahoma, determined to make writing his career. He wrote a fight story bought by Standard Magazines that year and became acquainted with editor Leo

Margulies who was to play an important rôle later in L'Amour's life. "The Town No Guns Could Tame" in *New Western* (3/40) was his first published Western story.

During the Second World War L'Amour was drafted and ultimately served with the U.S. Army Transportation Corps in Europe. However, in the two years before he was shipped out, he managed to write a great many adventure stories for Standard Magazines. The first story he published in 1946, the year of his discharge, was a Western, "Law of the Desert Born" in *Dime Western* (4/46). A talk with Leo Margulies resulted in L'Amour's agreeing to write Western stories for the various Western pulp magazines published by Standard Magazines, a third of which appeared under the byline Jim Mayo, the name of a character in L'Amour's earlier adventure fiction. The proposal for L'Amour to write new Hopalong Cassidy novels came from Margulies who wanted to launch *Hopalong Cassidy's Western Magazine* to take advantage of the popularity William Boyd's old films and new television series were enjoying with a new generation. Doubleday & Company agreed to publish the pulp novelettes in hard cover books. L'Amour was paid $500 a story, no royalties, and he was assigned the house name Tex Burns. L'Amour read Clarence E. Mulford's books about the Bar-20 and based his Hopalong Cassidy on Mulford's original creation. Only two issues of the magazine appeared before it ceased publication. Doubleday felt that the Hopalong character had to appear exactly as William Boyd did in the films and on television and thus the novels in book form had to be revamped to meet with this requirement prior to publication.

L'Amour's first Western novel under his own byline was WESTWARD THE TIDE (World's Work, 1950). It was rejected by every American publisher to which it was submitted. World's Work paid a flat £75 without royalties for British Empire rights in perpetuity. L'Amour sold his first Western short story to a slick magazine a year later, "The Gift of Cochise" in *Collier's* (7/5/52). Robert Fellows and John Wayne purchased screen rights to this story from L'Amour for $4,000 and James Edward Grant, one of Wayne's favorite screenwriters, developed a script from it, changing L'Amour's Ches Lane to Hondo Lane. L'Amour retained the right to novelize Grant's screenplay, which differs substantially from his short story, and he was able to get an endorsement from Wayne to be used as a blurb, stating that HONDO was the finest Western Wayne had ever read. HONDO (Fawcett Gold Medal, 1953) by Louis L'Amour was released on the same day as the film, HONDO (Warner, 1953), with a first printing of 320,000 copies.

With SHOWDOWN AT YELLOW BUTTE (Ace, 1953) by Jim Mayo, L'Amour began a series of short Western novels for Don Wollheim that could be doubled with other short novels by other authors in Ace Publishing's paperback two-fers. Advances on these were $800 and usually the author never earned any royalties. HELLER WITH A GUN (Fawcett Gold Medal, 1955) was the first of a series of original Westerns L'Amour had agreed to write under his own name following the success for Fawcett of HONDO. L'Amour wanted even this early to have his Western novels published in hard cover editions. He expanded "Guns of the Timberland" by Jim Mayo in *West* (9/50) for GUNS OF THE TIMBERLANDS (Jason Press, 1955), a hard cover Western for which he was paid an advance of $250. Another novel for Jason Press followed and then SILVER CAÑON (Avalon Books, 1956) for Thomas Bouregy & Company.

The great turn in L'Amour's fortunes came about because of problems Saul David was having with his original paperback Westerns program at Bantam Books. Fred Glidden had been signed to a contract to produce two original paperback Luke Short Western novels a year for an advance of $15,000 each. It was a long-term contract but, in the first ten years of it, Fred only wrote six novels. Literary agent Marguerite Harper then persuaded Bantam that Fred's brother, Jon, could help fulfill the contract and Jon was signed for eight Peter Dawson Western novels. When Jon died suddenly before completing even one book for Bantam, Harper managed to engage a ghost writer at the Disney studios to write these eight "Peter Dawson" novels, beginning with THE SAVAGES (Bantam, 1959). They proved inferior to anything Jon had ever written and what sales they had seemed to be due only to the Peter Dawson name.

Saul David wanted to know from L'Amour if *he* could deliver two Western novels a year. L'Amour said he could, and he did. In fact, by 1962 this number was increased to three original paperback novels a year. The first L'Amour novel to appear under the Bantam contract was RADIGAN (Bantam, 1958).

Yet I feel that some of Louis L'Amour's finest work is to be found in his early magazine fiction. Several of those stories are collected here, reprinted as they first appeared, and possessing the characteristics in purest form that I suspect account in largest measure for the loyal following Louis L'Amour won from his readers: the young male hero who is in the process of growing into manhood and who is evaluating other human beings and his own experiences; a resourceful frontier woman who has beauty as well as fortitude; and the powerful, romantic, strangely compelling vision of the American West that invests L'Amour's Western fiction and makes it such a delightful escape from the cares of a later time—in this author's words, that "big country needing big men and women to live in it" and where there was no place for "the frightened or the mean."

MISTAKES CAN KILL YOU

Ma Redlin looked up from the stove. "Where's Sam? He still out yonder?"

Johnny rubbed his palms on his chaps. "He ain't comin' to supper, Ma. He done rode off."

Pa and Else were watching him, and Johnny saw the hard lines of temper around Pa's mouth and eyes. Ma glanced at him apprehensively, but when Pa did not speak, she looked to her cooking. Johnny walked around the table and sat down across from Else.

When Pa reached for the coffee pot, he looked over at Johnny. "Was he alone, boy? Or did he ride off with that no-account Albie Bower?"

It was in Johnny neither to lie nor to carry tales. Reluctantly he replied: "He was with somebody. I reckon I couldn't be sure who it was."

Redlin snorted and put down his cup. It was a sore point with Joe Redlin that his son and only child should take up with the likes of Albie Bower. Back in Pennsylvania and Ohio the Redlins had been good God-fearing folk, while Bower was no good, and came from a no-good outfit. Lately he had been flashing money around, but he claimed to have won it gambling at Degner's Four Star Saloon.

"Once more I'll tell him," Redlin said harshly.

15

"I'll have no son of mine traipsin' with that Four Star outfit. Pack of thieves, that's what they are."

Ma looked up worriedly. She was a buxom woman with a round apple-cheeked face. Good humor was her normal manner. "Don't you be sayin' that away from home, Joe Redlin. That Loss Degner is a gunslinger, and he'd like nothin' so much as to shoot you after you takin' Else from him."

"I ain't afeerd of him." Redlin's voice was flat. Johnny knew that what he said was true. Joe Redlin was not afraid of Degner, but he avoided him, for Redlin was a small rancher, a one-time farmer, and not a fighting man. Loss Degner was bad all through and made no secret of it. His Four Star was the hang-out for all the tough element, and Degner had killed two men since Johnny had been in the country, as well as pistol-whipping a half dozen more.

It was not Johnny's place to comment, but secretly he knew the older Redlin was right. Once he had even gone so far as to warn Sam, but it only made the older boy angry.

Sam was almost twenty-one and Johnny but seventeen, but Sam's family had protected him and he had lived always close to the competence of Pa Redlin. Johnny had been doing a man's work since he was thirteen, fighting a man's battles, and making his own way in a hard world.

Johnny also knew what only Else seemed to

guess, that it was Hazel, Degner's red-haired singer, who drew Sam Redlin to the Four Star. It was rumored that she was Degner's woman, and Johnny had said as much to Sam. The younger Redlin had flown into a rage and, whirling on Johnny, had drawn back his fist. Something in Johnny's eyes stopped him, and, although Sam would never have admitted it, he was suddenly afraid.

Like Else, Johnny had been adrift when he came to the B Bar. Half dead with pneumonia, he had come up to the door on his black gelding, and the Redlins' hospitality had given him a bed and the best care the frontier could provide, and, when Johnny was well, he went to work to repay them. Then he stayed on for the spring roundup as a forty-a-month hand.

He volunteered no information, and they asked him no questions. He was slightly built and below medium height, but broad-shouldered and wiry. His shock of chestnut hair always needed cutting, and his green eyes held a lurking humor. He moved with deceptive slowness, but he was quick at work, and skillful with his hands. Nor did he wait to be told about things, for even before he began riding, he had mended the buckboard, cleaned out and shored up the spring, repaired the door hinges, and cleaned all the guns.

"We collect from Walters tomorrow," Redlin

said suddenly. "Then I'm goin' to make a payment on that Sprague place and put Sam on it. With his own place he'll straighten up and go to work."

Johnny stared at his plate, his appetite gone. He knew what that meant, for it had been in Joe Redlin's mind that Sam should marry Else and settle on that place. Johnny looked up suddenly, and his throat tightened as he looked at her. The gray eyes caught his, searched them for an instant, and then moved away, and Johnny watched the lamplight in her ash blonde hair, turning it to old gold.

He pushed back from the table and excused himself, going out into the moonlit yard. He lived in a room he had built into a corner of the barn. They had objected at first, wanting him to stay at the house, but he could not bear being close to Else, and then he had the lonely man's feeling for seclusion. Actually it had other advantages, for it kept him near his horse, and he never knew when he might want to ride on.

That black gelding and his new .44 Winchester had been the only incongruous notes in his getup when he arrived at the B Bar, for he had hidden his guns and his best clothes in a cave up the mountain, riding down to the ranch in shabby range clothes with only the .44 Winchester for safety.

He had watched the ranch for several hours

despite his illness before venturing down to the door. It paid to be careful, and there were men about who might know him.

Later, when securely in his own room, he had returned to his cache and dug out the guns and brought his outfit down to the ranch. Yet nobody had ever seen him with guns on, nor would they, if he was lucky.

The gelding turned its head and nickered at him, rolling its eyes at him. Johnny walked into the stall and stood there, one hand on the horse's neck. "Little bit longer, boy, then we'll go. You sit tight now."

There was another reason why he should leave now, for he had learned from Sam that Flitch was in town. Flitch had been on the Gila during the fight, and he had been a friend of Card Wells, who Johnny had killed at Picacho. Moreover, Flitch had been in Cimarron a year before that when Johnny, only fifteen then, had evened the score with the men who had killed his father and stolen their outfit. Johnny had gunned two of them down and put the third into the hospital.

Johnny was already on the range when Sam Redlin rode away the next morning to make his collection. Pa Redlin rode out with Else and found Johnny branding a yearling. Pa waved and rode on, but Else sat on her horse and watched him. "You're a good hand, Johnny," she said when he released the calf. "You should have your own outfit."

"That's what I want most," he admitted. "But I reckon I'll never have it."

"You can if you want it enough. Is it because of what's behind you?"

He looked up quickly then. "What do you know of me?"

"Nothing, Johnny, but what you've told us. But once, when I started into the barn for eggs, you had your shirt off and I saw those bullet scars. I know bullet scars because my own father had them. And you've never told us anything, which usually means there's something you aren't anxious to tell."

"I guess you're right." He tightened the girth on his saddle. "There ain't much to tell, though. I come West with my pa, and he was a lunger. I drove the wagon myself after we left Independence. Clean to Caldwell, then on to Santa Fe. We got us a little outfit with what Pa had left, and some mean fellers stole it off us, and they killed Pa."

Joe Redlin rode back to join them as Johnny was swinging into the saddle. He turned and glanced down at the valley. "Reckon that range won't get much use, Johnny," he said anxiously, "and the stock sure need it. Fair to middlin' grass, but too far to water."

"That draw, now," Johnny suggested. "I've

been thinkin' about that draw. It would take a sight of work, but a couple of good men with teams and some elbow grease could build them a dam across that draw. There's a sight of water comes down when it rains, enough to last most of the summer if it was dammed. Maybe even the whole year."

The three horses started walking toward the draw, and Johnny pointed out what he meant. "A feller over to Mobeetie did that one time," he said, "and it washed his dam out twice, but the third time she held, and he had him a little lake, all the year around."

"That's a good idea, Johnny." Redlin studied the set-up and then nodded. "A right good idea."

"Sam and me could do it," Johnny suggested, avoiding Pa Redlin's eyes.

Pa Redlin said nothing, but both Johnny and Else knew that Sam was not exactly ambitious about extra work. He was a good hand, Sam was, strong and capable, but he was big-headed about things and was little inclined to sticking with a job.

"Reminds me," Pa said, glancing at the sun. "Sam should be back soon."

"He might stop in town," Else suggested, and was immediately sorry she had said it for she could see the instant worry on Redlin's face. The idea of Sam Redlin stopping at the Four Star with $7,000 on him was scarcely a pleasant one.

21

Murder had been done there for much, much less. And then Sam was overconfident. He was even cocky.

"I reckon I'd better ride in and meet him," Redlin said, genuinely worried now. "Sam's a good boy, but he sets too much store by himself. He figures he can take care of himself anywhere, but that pack of wolves. . . ." His voice trailed off to silence.

Johnny turned in his saddle. "Why, I could just as well ride in, Pa," he said casually. "I ain't been to town for a spell, and, if anything happened, I could lend a hand."

Pa Redlin was about to refuse, but Else spoke up quickly. "Let him go, Pa. He could do some things for me, too, and Johnny's got a way with folks. Chances are he could get Sam back without trouble."

That's right! Johnny's thoughts were grim. *Send me along to save your boy. You don't care if I get shot, just so's he's been saved. Well, all right, I'll go. When I come back, I'll climb my gelding and light out. Up to Oregon. I've never been to Oregon.*

Flitch was in town. His mouth tightened a little, but at that it would be better than Pa's going. Pa always said the wrong thing, being outspoken like. He was a man who spoke his mind, and to speak one's mind to Flitch or Loss Degner would mean a shooting. It might be he

22

could get Sam out of town all right. If he was drinking, it would be hard. Especially if that redhead had her hands on him.

"You reckon you could handle it?" Pa asked doubtfully.

"Sure," Johnny said, his voice a shade hard, "I can handle it. I doubt if Sam's in any trouble. Later, maybe. All he'd need is somebody to side him."

"Well," Pa was reluctant, "better take your Winchester. My six-gun, too."

"You hang onto it. I'll make out."

Johnny turned the gelding and started back toward the ranch, his eyes cold. Seventeen he might be, but four years on the frontier on your own make pretty much of a man out of you. He didn't want any more shooting, but he had six men dead on his back trail now, not counting Comanches and Kiowas. Six, and he was seventeen. Next thing, they would be comparing him to Billy the Kid or to Wes Hardin.

He wanted no gunfighter's name, only a little spread of his own where he could run a few cows and raise horses, good stock, like some he had seen in east Texas. No range ponies for him, but good blood. That Sprague place now . . . but that was Sam's place, or as good as his. Well, why not? Sam was getting Else, and it was little enough he could do for Pa and Ma, to bring Sam home safe.

He left the gelding at the water trough and walked into the barn. In his room he dug some saddle gear away from a corner and, out of a hiding place in the corner, he took his guns. After a moment's thought, he took but one of them, leaving the .44 Russian behind. He didn't want to go parading into town with two guns on him, looking like a sure-enough shooter. Besides, with only one gun and the change in him, Flitch might not spot him at all.

Johnny was at the gate, riding out, when Else rode up. Else looked at him, her eyes falling to the gun on his hip. Her face was pale and her eyes large. "Be careful, Johnny. I had to say that because you know how hot-headed Pa is. He'd get killed, and he might get Sam killed."

That was true enough, but Johnny was aggrieved. He looked her in the eyes. "Sure, that's true, but you didn't think of Sam, now, did you? You were just thinking of Pa."

Her lips parted to protest, but then her face seemed to stiffen. "No, Johnny, it wasn't only Pa I thought of. I did think of Sam. Why shouldn't I?"

That was plain enough. Why shouldn't she? Wasn't she going to marry him? Wasn't Sam getting the Sprague place when they got that money back safe?

He touched his horse lightly with a spur and moved on past her. All right, he would send Sam back to her, if he could. It was time he was moving on, anyway.

The gelding liked the feel of the trail and moved out fast. Ten miles was all, and he could do that easy enough, and so he did it, and Johnny turned the black horse into the street and stopped before the livery stable, swinging down. Sam's horse was tied at the Four Star's hitch rail. The saddlebags were gone.

Johnny studied the street, and then crossed it and walked down along the buildings on the same side as the Four Star. He turned quickly in to the door.

Sam Redlin was sitting at a table with the red-head, the saddlebags on the table before him, and he was drunk. He was very drunk. Johnny's eyes swept the room. The bartender and Loss Degner were standing together, talking. Neither of them paid any attention to Johnny, for neither knew him. But Flitch did.

Flitch was standing down the bar with Albie Bower, but none of the old Gila River outfit. Both of them looked up, and Flitch kept looking, never taking his eyes from Johnny. Something bothered him, and maybe it was the one gun.

Johnny moved over to Sam's table. They had to get out of here fast, before Flitch remembered. "Hi, Sam," he said. "Just happened to be in town, and Pa said, if I saw you, to side you on the way home."

Sam stared at him sullenly. "Side me? You?" He snorted his contempt. "I need no man to side me. You can tell Pa I'll be home later tonight." He glanced at the redhead. "Much later."

"Want I should carry this stuff home for you?" Johnny put his hand on the saddlebags.

"Leave him be," Hazel protested angrily. "Can't you see he don't want to be bothered? He's capable of takin' care of himself, an' he don't need no kid for gardeen."

"Beat it," Sam said. "You go on home. I'll come along later."

"Better come now, Sam." Johnny was getting worried, for Loss Degner had started for the table.

"Here, you." Degner was sharp. "Leave that man alone. He's a friend of mine, and I'll have no saddle tramp annoying my customers."

Johnny turned on him. "I'm no saddle tramp. I ride for his pa. He asked me to ride home with him . . . now. That's what I aim to do."

As he spoke, he was not thinking of Degner, but of Flitch. The gunman was behind him now, and neither Flitch, fast as he was, nor Albie Bower was above shooting a man in the back.

"I said to beat it." Sam stared at him drunkenly. "Saddle tramp's what you are. Folks never should have took you in."

"That's it," Degner said. "Now get out. He don't want you nor your company."

26

There was a movement behind him, and he heard Flitch say: "Loss, let me have him. I know this *hombre*. This is that kid gunfighter, Johnny O'Day, from the Gila."

Johnny turned slowly, his green eyes flat and cold.

"Hello, Flitch. I heard you were around." Carefully he moved away from the table, aware of the startled look on Hazel's face, the suddenly tight awareness on the face of Loss Degner. "You lookin' for me, Flitch?" It was a chance he had to take. His best chance now. If shooting started, he might grab the saddlebags and break for the door and then the ranch. They would be through with Sam Redlin once the money was gone.

"Yeah." Flitch stared at him, his unshaven face hard with the lines of evil and shadowed by the intent that rode him hard. "I'm lookin' for you. Always figured you got off easy, made you a fast rep gunnin' down your betters."

Bower had moved up beside him, but Loss Degner had drawn back to one side. Johnny's eyes never left Flitch. "You in this, Loss?"

Degner shrugged. "Why should I be? I was no Gila River gunman. This is your quarrel. Finish it between you."

"All right, Flitch," Johnny said. "You want it. I'm givin' you your chance to start the play."

The stillness of a hot mid-afternoon lay on the

Four Star. A fly buzzed against the dusty, cob-webbed back window. Somewhere in the street a horse stamped restlessly, and a distant pump creaked. Flitch stared at him, his little eyes hard and bright. His sweat-stained shirt was torn at the shoulder, and there was dust ingrained in the pores of his face.

His hands dropped in a flashing draw, but he had only cleared leather when Johnny's first bullet hit him, puncturing the Bull Durham tag that hung from his shirt pocket. The second shot cut the edge of it, and the third, fourth, and fifth slammed into Albie Bower, knocking him back step by step, but Albie's gun was hammering, and it took the sixth shot to put him down.

Johnny stood over them, staring down at their bodies, and then he turned to face Loss Degner.

Degner was smiling, and he held a gun in his hand from which a thin tendril of smoke lifted. Startled, Johnny's eyes flickered to Sam Redlin.

Sam lay across the saddlebags, blood trickling from his temples. He had been shot through the head by Degner under cover of the gun battle, murdered without a chance!

Johnny O'Day's eyes lifted to Loss Degner's. The saloonkeeper was still smiling. "Yes, he's dead, and I've killed him. He had it coming, the fool. Thinking we cared to listen to his bragging. All we wanted was that money, and now we've got it. Me . . . Hazel and I. We've got it."

"Not yet." Johnny's lips were stiff and his heart was cold. He was thinking of Pa, Ma, and Else. "I'm still here."

"You?" Degner laughed. "With an empty gun? I counted your shots, boy. Even Johnny O'Day is cold turkey with an empty gun. Six shots . . . two for Flitch, and beautiful shooting, too, but four shots for Albie, who was moving and shooting, not so easy a target. But now I've got you. With you dead, I'll just say Sam came here without any money, that he got shot during the fight. Sound good to you?"

Johnny still faced him, his gun in his hand. "Not bad," he said, "but you still have me here, Loss. And this gun ain't empty."

Degner's face tightened and then relaxed. "Not empty? I counted the shots, kid, so don't try bluffing me. Now I'm killing you." He tilted his gun toward Johnny O'Day, and Johnny fired once, twice . . . a third time. As each bullet hit him, Loss Degner jerked and twisted, but the shock of the wounds, and death wounds they were, was nothing to the shock of the bullets from that empty gun.

He sagged against the bar and then slipped toward the floor.

Johnny moved in on him. "You can hear me, Loss?" The killer's eyes lifted to his. "This ain't a six-shooter. It's a Watch twelve-shot Navy gun, thirty-six caliber. She's right handy, Loss,

29

and it only goes to show you shouldn't jump to conclusions."

Hazel sat at the table, staring at the dying Degner.

"You better go to him, Red," Johnny said quietly. "He's only got a minute."

She stared at him as he picked up the saddlebags and backed to the door.

Russell, the storekeeper, was on the steps with a half dozen others, none of whom he knew. "Degner killed Sam Redlin," he said. "Take care of Sam, will you?"

At Russell's nod, Johnny swung to the saddle and turned the gelding toward home.

He wouldn't leave now. He couldn't leave now. They would be all alone there, without Sam. Besides, Pa was going to need help on that dam. "Boy," he touched the gelding's neck, "I reckon we got to stick around for a while."

THE RIDER OF
THE RUBY HILLS

I

There was a lonely place where the trail ran up to the sky. It turned sharply left on the very point of a lofty promontory overlooking the long sweep of the valley below. Here the trail offered to the passerby a vision at this hour. Rosy-tipped peaks and distant purple mountains could be seen, beyond the far reach of the tall-grass range. Upon the very lip of the rocky shelf sat a solitary horseman. He was a man tall in the saddle, astride a strangely marked horse. Its head was held high, its ears were pricked forward with attention riveted upon the valley, as though in tune with the thoughts of its rider. Thoughts that said there lay a new country, with new dangers, new rewards, and new trails.

The rider was a tall man, narrow-hipped and powerful of chest and shoulder. His features were blunt and rugged, so that a watcher might have said: "Here is a man who is not handsome, but a fighter." Yet he was good-looking in his own hard, confident way. He looked now as Cortez might have looked upon a valley in Mexico.

He came alone and penniless, but he did not come as one seeking favors. He did not come hunting a job. He came as a conqueror. For Ross Haney had made his decision. At twenty-seven he was broke. He sat in the middle of all he owned, a splendid Appaloosa gelding, a fine California saddle, a .44 Winchester rifle, and two walnut-stocked Colt .44 pistols. These were his all. Behind him was a life that had taken him from a cradle in a covered wagon to the hurricane deck of many a hard-headed bronco.

It was a life that had left him rich in experience, but poor in goods of the world. The experience was the hard-fisted experience of cold winters, dry ranges, and the dusty bitterness of cattle drives. He had fought Comanches and rustlers, hunted buffalo and horse thieves. Now he was going to ride for himself, to fight for himself.

His keen dark eyes from under the flat black brim of his hat studied the country below with speculative glint. His judgment of terrain would have done credit to a general, and in his own way Ross Haney was a general. His arrival in the Ruby Valley country was in its way an invasion.

He was a young man with a purpose. He did not want wealth but a ranch, a well-watered ranch in a good stock country. That his pockets were empty did not worry him, for he had made up his mind, and, as men had discovered before this, Ross Haney with his mind made up was a force to be reckoned with. Nor was he riding blindly into a strange land. Like a good tactician he had gathered his information carefully, judged the situation, the terrain, and the enemy before he began his move.

This was a new country to him, but he knew the landmarks and the personalities. He knew the strength and the weaknesses of its rulers, knew the economic factors of their existence, knew the stresses and the strains within it. He knew that he rode into a valley at war—that blood had been shed, and that armed men rode its trails day and night. Into this land he rode a man alone, determined to have his own from the country, come what may, letting the chips fall where they might.

With a movement of his body he turned the gelding left down the trail into the pines, a trail where at this late hour it would soon be dark, a trail somber, majestic in its stillness under the columned trees.

As he moved under the trees, he removed his hat and rode slowly. It was good country, a country where a man could live and grow, and where, if he was lucky, he might have sons to grow tall and straight beside him. This he wanted. He wanted his own hearth fire, the creak of his own pump, the heads of his own horses looking over the gate bars for his hand to feed them. He wanted peace, and for it he came to a land at war.

A flicker of light caught his eye, and the faint smell of wood smoke. He turned the gelding toward the fire, and, when he was near, he swung down. The sun's last rays lay bright through the pines upon this spot. The earth was trampled by hoofs, and in the fire itself the ashes were gray but for one tiny flame that thrust a bright spear upward from the end of a stick.

Studying the scene, his eyes held for an instant on one place where the parched grass had been blackened in a perfect ring. His eyes glinted with hard humor. *A cinch-ring artist. Dropped her there to cool and she singed the grass. A pretty smooth gent, I'd say.* Not slick enough, of course. A smarter man, or a less confident one, would have pulled up that handful of blackened grass and tossed it into the flames.

There had been two men here, his eyes told him. Two men and two horses. One of the men had been a big man with small feet. The impressions of his feet were deeper and he had mounted the largest horse.

Curious, he studied the scene. This was a new country for him and it behooved a man to know the local customs. He grinned at the thought. If cinch-ring branding was one of the local customs, it was a strange one. In most sections of the country the activity was frowned upon, to say the least. If an artist was caught pursuing his calling, he was likely to find himself at the wrong end of a hair rope with nothing under his feet.

The procedure was simple enough. One took a cinch ring from his own saddle gear and, holding it between a couple of sticks, used it when red-hot like any other branding iron. A good hand with a cinch ring could easily duplicate any known brand, depending only upon his degree of skill.

Ross rolled and lighted a smoke. If he were found on the spot, it would require explaining, and at the moment he had no intention of explaining anything. He swung his leg over the saddle and turned the gelding downtrail once more.

Not three miles away lay the cow town known as Soledad. To his right, and about six miles away, was an imposing cluster of buildings shaded beneath a splendid grove of old cotton-woods. Somewhat nearer, and also well-shaded, was a smaller ranch.

Beyond the rocky ridge that stretched an anxious finger into the lush valley was Walt Pogue's Box N spread. The farther ranch belonged to Chalk Reynolds, his RR outfit being easily the biggest in the Ruby Hills country. The nearer ranch belonged to Bob and Sherry Vernon.

"When thieves fall out," Ross muttered aloud, "honest men get their dues. Or that's what they say. Now I'm not laying any claim to being so completely honest, but there's trouble brewing in this valley. When the battle smoke blows away,

Ross Haney is going to be top dog on one of those ranches. They've got it all down there. They have range, money, power. They have gun hands riding for them, but you and me, Río, we've only got each other."

He was a lone wolf on the prowl. Down there they ran in packs, and he would circle the packs, alone. When the moment came, he would close in.

"There's an old law, Río, that only the strong survive," he said. "Those ranches belong to men who were strong, and some of them still are. They were strong enough to take them from other men, from smaller men, weaker men. That's the story of Reynolds and Pogue. They rustled cows until they grew big and now they sit on the housetops and crow. Or they did until they began fightin' one another."

"Your reasoning"—the cool, quiet voice was feminine—"is logical, but dangerous. I might suggest that, when you talk to your horse, you should be sure his are the only ears!"

She sat well in the saddle, poised and alert. There was a quirk of humor at the corners of her mouth, and nothing of coyness or fear in her manner. Every inch of her showed beauty, care, and consideration of appearances that were new to him, but beneath them there were both fire and steel—and quality.

"That's good advice," he agreed, measuring her with his eyes. "Very good advice."

"Now that you've looked me over," she suggested coolly, "would you like to examine my teeth for age?"

He grinned, unabashed. "No, but now that I've looked you over, I'd say you are pretty much of a woman. The kind that's made for a man!"

She returned his glance, then smiled as if the remark had pleased her. So she changed the subject. "Just which ranch do you plan to be top dog on when the fighting is over?"

"I haven't decided," he said frankly. "I'm a right choosy sort of man when it comes to horses, ranches, and women!"

"Yes?" She glanced at the gelding. "I'd say your judgment of horses isn't obvious by that one. Not that he isn't well-shaped, and I imagine he could run, but you could do better."

"I doubt it." He glanced at her fine, clean-limbed thoroughbred. "I'd bet a little money he can outrun that beauty of yours, here to Soledad."

Her eyes flashed. "Why, you idiot! Flame is the fastest horse in this country. He comes of racing stock!"

"I don't doubt it," Haney agreed. "He's a fine horse. But I'll bet my saddle against a hundred dollars that this Appaloosa will kick dust in his face before we get to Soledad!"

She laughed scornfully, and her head came up. "You're on!" she cried, and her red horse gave a great bound and hit the trail running. That jump gave the bay the start, but Ross knew his gelding.

Leaning over, he yelled into the horse's ear as they charged after the bay: "Come on, boy! We've got to beat that bay! We need the money!" And Río, seeming to understand, stretched his legs and ran like a scared rabbit.

As they swept into the main road and in full sight of Soledad, the bay was leading by three lengths, but despite the miles behind it, the Appaloosa loved to run, and he was running now.

The gelding had blood of Arabians in his veins, and he was used to off-hand, cow camp style racing. The road took a small jog, but Ross did not swing the gelding around it, but took the desert and mountain-bred horse across the stones and through the mesquite, hitting the road scarcely a length behind the big red horse.

Men were gathering in the street and on the edge of town now and shouting about the racing horses. With a half mile to go the big red horse was slowing. He was a sprinter, but he had been living too well with too little running. The gelding was just beginning to run. Neck stretched, Ross leaning far forward to cut the wind resistance and lend impetus with his weight, the mustang thundered alongside the bay horse, and neck and neck they raced up to the town. Then, with the nearest building only a short jump ahead, Ross Haney spoke to the Appaloosa: "*Now,* Río! *Now!*"

With a lunge, the spotted horse was past and went racing into the street leading by a length.

Ross eased back on the reins and let the horse run on down the street abreast of the big red horse. They slowed to a canter, then a walk. The girl's eyes were wide and angry.

"You cheated! You cut across that bend!"

Ross chuckled. "You could have, miss! And you got off to a running start. Left me standing still!"

"I thought you wanted a race!" she protested scornfully. "You cheated me!"

Ross Haney drew up sharply, and his eyes went hard. "I reckon, ma'am," he said, "you come from a long line of sportsmen! You can forget the bet!"

The sarcasm in his voice cut like a whip. She opened her mouth to speak, but he had turned the Appaloosa away and was walking it back toward the center of town.

For an instant, she started to follow, and then with a toss of her head, she let him go.

II

Several men were standing in front of the livery stable when he rode up. They looked at his horse, then at him. "That's a runner you got there, stranger! I reckon Sherry Vernon didn't relish getting beat! She sets great store by the Flame horse!"

Haney swung down and led the horse into the stable where he rubbed him down and fed him. As he worked, he thought over what he had just learned. The girl was Sherry Vernon, one of the owners of the Twin V spread, and she had overheard his meditations on his plans. How seriously she would take them would be something else again. Well, it did not matter. He was planning no subterfuge. He had come to Ruby Valley on the prod, and they could find it out now as well as later.

The girl had been beautiful. That stuck in his mind after he thought of all the rest. It was the feeling that hung over his thinking with a certain aura that disturbed him. He had known few women who affected him, and those few had been in New Orleans or Kansas City on his rare trips there. Yet this one touched a chord that had answered to none of the others.

Suddenly he was conscious of a looming figure beside him. For a moment he continued to work.

Then he looked around into a broad, handsome face. The man was smiling.

"My name's Pogue," he said, thrusting out a hand. "Walt Pogue. I own the Box N. Is that horse for sale?"

"No, he's not."

"I'd not figured you'd be willing to sell. If you get that idea, come look me up. I'll give you five hundred for him."

$500? That was a lot of money in a country full of ten-dollar mustangs or where a horse was often traded for a quart of whiskey.

"No," Haney repeated, "he's not for sale."

"Lookin' for a job? I could use a hand."

Ross Haney drew erect and looked over the horse's back. He noticed, and the thought somehow irritated him, that Pogue was even bigger than himself. The rancher was all of three inches taller and forty pounds heavier. And he did not look fat.

"Gun hand? Or cowhand?"

Walt Pogue's eyes hardened a shade, and then he smiled, a grim knowing smile. "Why, man," he said softly, "that would depend on you. But if you hire on as a warrior, you've got to be good!"

"I'm good. As good as any you've got."

"As good as Bob Streeter or Repp Hanson?"

Ross Haney's expression made no change, but within him he felt something tighten up and turn hard and wary. If Pogue had hired Streeter and

Hanson, this was going to be ugly. Both men were killers, and not particular how they worked or how they killed.

"As good as Streeter or Hanson?" Haney shrugged. "A couple of cheap killers. Blood hunters. They aren't fighting men." His dark eyes met that searching stare of Walt Pogue again. "Who does Reynolds have?"

Pogue's face seemed to lower and he stared back at Haney. "He's got Emmett Chubb."

Emmett Chubb! So? And after all these years? "He won't have him long," Haney said, "because I'm going to kill him!"

Triumph leaped in Pogue's eyes. Swiftly he moved around the horse. "Haney," he said, "that job could get you an even thousand dollars."

"I don't take money for killing snakes."

"You do that job within three days and you'll get a thousand dollars," Pogue said flatly.

Ross Haney pushed by the big man without replying and walked into the street. Three men sat on the rail by the stable door. Had they heard what was said inside? He doubted it, and yet?

Across the street and three doors down was the Trail Emporium. For a long moment his eyes held their look at the one light gleaming in the back of the store. It was after hours and the place was closed, but at the back door there might be a chance. Deliberately he stepped into the street and crossed toward the light.

Behind him Walt Pogue moved into the doorway and stared after him, his brow furrowed with thought. His eyes went down the lean, powerful figure of the strange rider with a puzzled expression. Who was he? Where had he come from? Why was he here? He wore two well-worn, tied-down guns. He had the still, remote face and the careful eyes typical of a man who had lived much with danger, and typical of so many of the gunfighters of the West. He had refused, or avoided the offer of a job, yet he had seemed well aware of conditions in the valley. Had Reynolds sent for him? Or Bob Vernon? He had ridden into town racing with Sherry. Had they met on the trail, or come from the V V? That Pogue must know and at once. If Bob Vernon was hiring gun hands, it would mean trouble, and that he did not want. One thing at a time. Where was he going now? Resisting an instinct to follow Haney, Pogue turned and walked up the street toward the Bit and Bridle Saloon.

Haney walked up to the back door of the store building, hesitated an instant, then tapped lightly.

Footsteps sounded within, and he heard the sound of a gun being drawn from a scabbard. "Who's there?"

Haney spoke softly. "A rider from the Pecos."

The door opened at once, and Ross slid through the opening. The man who faced him was round and white-haired. Yet the eyes that took Haney in from head to heel were not old eyes. They were shrewd, hard, and knowing.

"Coffee?"

"Sure. Food, if you got some ready."

"About to eat myself." The man placed the gun on a sideboard and lifted the coffee pot from the stove. He filled the cup as Ross dropped into a chair. "Who sent you here?"

Haney glanced up, then tipped back in his chair. "Don't get on the prod, old-timer. I'm friendly. When an old friend of yours heard I was headed this way, and might need a smart man to give me a word of advice, he told me to look you up. And he told me what to say to you, Scott."

"My days on that trail are over."

"Mine never started. This is a business trip. I'm planning to locate in the valley."

"Locate? Here?" The older man stared at him. He filled his own cup, and, dishing up a platter of food and slapping bread on a plate, he sat down. "You came to me for advice. All right, you'll get it. Get on your horse and ride out of here as fast as you can. This is no country for strangers, and there have been too many of them around. Things are due to bust wide open and there will be a sight of killin' before it's over."

"You're right, of course."

"Sure. An' after it's over, what's left for a gun hand? You can go on the owlhoot, that's all. The very man who hired you and paid you warrior's wages won't want you when the fighting is over. There's revolution coming in this country. If you know the history of revolutions, you'll know that as soon as one is over the first thing they do is liquidate the revolutionists. You ride out of here."

Ross Haney ate in silence. The older man was right. To ride out would be the intelligent, sensible, and safe course, and he had absolutely no intention of doing it.

"Scott, I didn't come here to hire on as a gun hand. In fact, I have already had an offer. I came into this country because I've sized it up and I know what it's like. This country can use a good man, a strong man. There's a place for me here, and I mean to take it. Also, I want a good ranch. I aim to settle down, and I plan to get my ranch the same way Pogue, Reynolds, and the rest of them got theirs."

"Force? You mean with a gun?" Scott was incredulous. "Listen, young fellow, Pogue has fifty riders on his range, and most of them are ready to fight at the drop of a hat. Reynolds has just as many, and maybe more. And you come in here alone . . . or are you alone?"

The storekeeper bent a piercing gaze upon the young man, who smiled.

"I'm alone." Haney shrugged. "Scott, I've been fighting for existence ever since I was big enough to walk. I've fought to hold other people's cattle, fought for other men's homes, fought for the lives of other men. I've worked and bled and sweated my heart out in rain, dust, and storm. Now I want something for myself. Maybe I came too late. Maybe I'm 'way off the trail. But it seems to me that, when trouble starts, a man might stand on the sidelines, and, when the time comes, he might move in. You see, I know how Walt Pogue got his ranch. Vin Carter was a friend of mine until Emmett Chubb killed him. He told me how Pogue forced his old man off his range and took over. Well, I happen to know that none of this range is legally held. It's been preëmpted, which gives them a claim, of course. Well, I've got a few ideas myself. And I'm moving in."

"Son"—Scott leaned across the table—"listen to me. Pogue's the sort of man who would hire killers by the hundreds if he had to. He did force Carter off his range. He did take it by force, and he has held it by force. Now he and Chalk are in a battle over who is to keep it, and which one is to come out on top. The Vernons are the joker in the deck. What both Reynolds and Pogue want is the Vernon place because whoever holds it has a grip on this country. But both of them are taking the Vernons too lightly. They have something up their sleeve, or somebody has."

"What do you mean?"

"There's this Star Levitt, for one. He's no soft

touch, that one! And then he's got some riders around there, and I'd say they do more work for him than for the Vernon spread . . . and not all honest work, by any means."

"Levitt a Western man?"

"He could be. Probably is. But whoever he is, he knows his way around an' he's one sharp *hombre*. Holds his cards close to his chest, an' plays 'em that way. He's the one you've got to watch in this deal, not Reynolds or Pogue."

Ross Haney leaned back in his chair and smiled at Scott. "That meal sure tasted good," he acknowledged. "Now comes the rough part. I want to borrow some money . . . military funds," he added, grinning.

Scott shook his white head. "You sure beat all! You come into this country huntin' trouble, all alone, an' without money! You've got nerve! I only hope you've got the gun savvy and the brains to back it up." The blue eyes squinted from his leather brown face and he smiled. He was beginning to like Haney. The tall young man had humor and the nerve of the project excited and amused the old outlaw. "How much to you want?"

"A hundred dollars."

"That all? You won't get far in this country on that."

"No, along with it I want some advice." Haney hitched himself forward and took a bit of paper from his pocket, then a stub of pencil. Then from a leather folder he took a larger sheet that he unfolded carefully. It was a beautifully tanned piece of calfskin, and on it was drawn a map. Carefully he moved the dishes aside and placed it on the table facing the older man. "Look that over and, if you see any mistakes, correct me."

Scott stared at the map, then he leaned forward, his eyes indicating his amazed interest. It was a map, drawn to scale and in amazing detail, of the Ruby Hills country. Every line camp, every water hole, every ranch, and every stand of trees was indicated plainly. Distances were marked on straight lines between the various places, and heights of land. Lookout points were noted, cañons indicated. Studying the map, Scott could find nothing it had missed.

Slowly he leaned back in his chair. When he looked up, his expression was halfway between respect and worry. "Son, where did you get that map?"

"Get it? I made it. I drew it myself, Scott. For three years I've talked to every 'puncher or other man I've met from this country. As they told me stuff, I checked with others and built this map. You know how Western men are. Most of them are pretty good at description. A man down in the Live Oaks country who never left it knows how the sheriff looks in Julesberg, and exactly where the corrals are in Dodge." Haney took a deep breath, then continued his story. "Well, I've been studying this situation quite a spell. An old buffalo hunter and occasional trapper was in this country once, and he told me about it when I was a kid. It struck me as a place I'd like to live, so I planned accordingly. I learned all I could about it, rode for outfits oftentimes just because some 'puncher on the spread had worked over here. Then I ran into Vin Carter. He was born here. He told me all about it, and I got more from him than any of them. While I was riding north with a herd of cattle, Emmett Chubb moved in, picked a fight with the kid, and killed him. And I think Walt Pogue paid him to do it. So it goes further than the fact that I'm range hungry, and I'll admit I am. I want my own spread. But Vin rode with me and we fought sandstorms and blizzards together from Texas to Montana and back. So I'm a man on the prod. Before I get through, I'll own me a ranch in this country, a nice ranch with nice buildings, and then I'll get a wife and settle down."

Scott's eyes glinted. "It's a big order, son. Gosh, if I was twenty years younger, I'd throw in with you. I sure would."

"There's no man I'd want more, Scott, but this is my fight, and I'll make it alone. You can stake me to eating money, if you want, and I'll need some Forty-Four cartridges."

The older man nodded assent. "You can have them, an' willin'. Have you got a plan?"

51

Haney nodded. "It's already started. I've filed on Thousand Springs."

Scott came off his chair, his face a mask of incredulity. "You *what?*"

"I filed a claim, an' I've staked her out and started to prove up." Ross was smiling over his coffee, enjoying Scott's astonishment.

"But, man! That's sheer suicide! That's right in the middle of Chalk's best range! That water hole is worth a fortune. A dozen fortunes. That's what half the fighting is about."

"I know it." Haney was calm. "I knew that before I came in here. That Appaloosa of mine never moved a step until I had my plan of action all staked out. And I bought the Bullhorn."

This time astonishment was beyond the storekeeper. "How could you buy it? Gov'ment land, ain't it?"

"No. That's what they all think. Even Vin Carter thought so, but it was part of a Spanish Grant. I found that out by checking through some old records. So I hunted up a Mex down in the Big Bend country who owned it. I bought it from him, bought three hundred acres, taking in the whole Bullhorn headquarters spread, the water hole, and the cliffs in back of it. That includes most of that valley where Pogue cuts his meadow hay."

"Well, I'm forever bushed. If that don't beat all." Scott tapped thoughtfully with his pipe bowl.

Then he looked up. "What about Hitson Spring?"

"That's another thing I want to talk to you about. You own it."

"I do, eh? How did you come to think that?"

"Met an old sidewinder down in Laredo named Smite Emmons. He was pretty drunk one night in a greaser's shack, and he told me how foolish you were to file claim on that land. Said you could have bought it from the Indians just as cheap."

Scott chuckled. "I did. I bought it from the Indians, too. Believe me, son, nobody around here knows that. It would be a death sentence."

"Then sell it to me. I'll give you my note for five thousand right now."

"Your note, eh?" Scott chuckled. "Son, you'd better get killed. It will be cheaper to bury you than pay up." He tapped his pipe bowl again. "Tell you what I'll do. I'll take your note for five hundred and the fun of watching what happens."

Solemnly Ross Haney wrote out a note, and handed it to Scott. The old man chuckled as he read it.

I hereby agree to pay on or before the 15th of March, 1877, to Westbrook Scott, the sum of $500 and the fun of watching what happens for the 160 acres of land known as Hitson Spring.

"All right, son. Sign her up. I'll get you the deed."

III

When Ross had pocketed the two papers, the deed from the government to Scott and deeded over to him, and the skin deed from the Comanches, the old man sat up and reached for the coffee pot.

"You know what you've done? You've got a claim on the three best sources of water in Ruby Valley, the only three that are sure-fire all the year around. And what will they do when they find out? They'll kill you!"

"They won't find out for a while. I'm not talking until the fight's been taken out of them."

"What about your claim stakes at Thousand Springs?"

"Buried. Iron stakes, and driven deep into the ground. There's sod and grass over the top."

"What about proving up?"

"That, too. You know how that spring operates? Actually it is one great big spring back inside the mountain, flowing out through the rocky face of the cliff in hundreds of tiny rivulets. Well, atop the mesa there is a good piece of land that falls into my claim, and back in the woods there is some land I can plow. I've already broken that land, smoothed her out, and put in a crop. I've got a trail to the top of that mesa, and a stone house built up there. I'm in business, Scott!"

Scott looked at him and shook his head. Then he pushed back from the table and, getting up, went into the store. When he returned, he had several boxes of shells.

"In the mornin' come around and stock up," he suggested. "You better make you a cache or two with an extra gun here and there, and some extra ammunition. Maybe a little grub. Be good insurance, and, son, you'll need it."

"That's good advice. I'll do it, an' you keep track of the expense. I'll settle every cent of it when this is over."

With money in his pocket he walked around the store and crossed the street to the Bit and Bridle. The bartender glanced at him, then put a bottle and a glass in front of him. He was a short man, very thick and fat, but, after a glance at the corded forearms, Ross was very doubtful about it all being fat.

A couple of lazy-talking cowhands held down the opposite end of the bar, and there was a poker game in progress at a table. Several other men sat around on chairs. They were the usual nondescript crowd of the cow trails.

He poured his drink, and had just taken it between his thumb and fingers when the bat-wing doors thrust open and he heard the click of heels behind him. He neither turned nor looked around. The amber liquid in the glass held his attention. He had never been a drinking man, taking only occasional shots, and he was not going to drink much tonight.

The footsteps halted abreast of him, and a quick, clipped voice said in very precise words: "Are you the chap who owns that fast horse, the one with the black forequarters and the white over the loin and hips?"

He glanced around, turning his head without moving his body. There was no need to tell him that this was Bob Vernon. He was a tall, clean-limbed young man who was like her in that imperious lift to his chin, unlike her in his quick, decisive manner.

"There's spots, egg-shaped black spots over the white," said Haney. "That the one you mean?"

"My sister is outside. She wants to speak to you."

"I don't want to speak to her. You can tell her that." He turned his attention to his drink.

What happened then happened so fast it caught him off balance. A hand grasped him by the shoulder and spun him around in a grip of iron, and he was conscious of being surprised at the strength in that slim hand. Bob Vernon was staring at him, his eyes blazing.

"I said my sister wanted to speak to you!"

"And I said I didn't want to speak to her." Ross Haney's voice was slow-paced and even. "Now take your hand off me and don't ever lay a hand on me again."

Bob Vernon was a man who had never backed down for anyone. From the East he had come into the cow country of Ruby Valley and made a place for himself by energy, decision, and his own youthful strength. Yet he had never met a man such as he faced now. As he looked into the hard eyes of the stranger, he felt something turn over deeply inside him. It was as though he had parted the brush and looked into the face of a lion.

Vernon dropped his hand. "I'm sorry. I'm afraid your manner made me forgetful. My sister can't come into a place like this."

The two men measured each other, and the suddenly alert audience in the Bit and Bridle let their eyes go from Vernon to the stranger. Bob Vernon they knew well enough to know he was afraid of nothing that walked. They also knew his normal manner was polite to a degree rarely encountered in the West where manners were inclined to be brusque, friendly, and lacking in formality. Yet there was something else between these two now. As one man they seemed to sense the same intangible something that had touched Bob Vernon.

The bat-wing doors parted suddenly, and Sherry Vernon stepped into the room.

First, Haney was aware of a shock that such a girl could come into such a place, and, second, of shame that he had been the cause. Then he felt admiration sweep over him at her courage.

Beautiful in a gray, tailored riding habit, her head lifted proudly, she walked up to Ross Haney. Her face was set and her eyes were bright.

Ross was suddenly conscious that never in all his life had he looked into eyes so fine, so filled with feeling.

"Sir"—and her voice could be heard in every corner of the room—"I do not know what your name may be, but I have come to pay you your money. Your horse beat Flame today, and beat him fairly. I regret the way I acted, but it was such a shock to have Flame beaten that I allowed you to get away without being paid. I am very sorry. However," she added quickly, "if you would like to run against Flame again, I'll double the bet."

"Thank you, Miss Vernon." He bowed slightly, from the hips. "It was only that remark about my horse that made me run him at all. You see, miss, as you no doubt know, horses have feelin's. I couldn't let you run down my horse to his face thataway!"

Her eyes were on his and, suddenly, they crinkled at the corners and her lips rippled with a little smile.

"Now, if you'll allow me. . . ." He took her arm and escorted her from the room. Inside, they heard a sudden burst of applause, and he smiled as he offered her his hands for her foot. She stepped into them, then swung into her position on the horse.

"I'm sorry you had to come in there, but your brother was kind of abrupt."

"That's quite all right," she replied quickly, almost too quickly. "Now our business is completed."

He stepped back and watched them ride away into the darkness of early evening. Then he turned back to the saloon. He almost ran into a tall, carefully dressed man who had walked up behind him. A man equally as large as Pogue.

Pale blue eyes looked from a handsome, perfectly cut face of city white. He was trim, neat, and precise. Only the guns at his hips looked deadly with their polished butts and worn holsters.

"That," said the tall man, gesturing after Sherry Vernon, "is a staked claim!"

Ross Haney was getting angry. Men who were bigger than he always irritated him, anyway. "If you think you can stake a claim on any woman, you've got a lot to learn."

He shoved by toward the door, but behind him the voice said: "But that one's staked. You hear me?"

Soledad by night was a tiny scattering of lights along the dark river of the street. Music from the tinny piano in the Bit and Bridle drifted down the street, and with it the lazy voice of someone singing a cow camp song. Ross Haney turned up the street toward the two-story frame hotel, his mind unable to free itself from the vision that was Sherry Vernon.

For the first time, the wife who was to share that ranch had a face. Until now there had been in his thoughts the vague shadow of a personality and a character, but there had been no definite features, nothing that could be recognized. Now, after seeing Sherry, he knew there could be but one woman in the ranch house he planned to build.

He smiled wryly as he thought of her sharing his life. What would she think of a cowhand? A drifting gun hand? And what would she say when it became known that he was Ross Haney? Not that the name meant very much, for it did not. Only, in certain quarters where fighting men gather, he had acquired something of a reputation. The stories about him had drifted across the country as such stories will, and, while he had little notoriety as a gunfighter, he was known as a hard, capable man who would and could fight.

He was keenly aware of his situation in Soledad and the Ruby Hills country. As yet, he was an outsider. They were considering him, and Pogue had already sensed enough of what he was to offer a job, gun or saddle job. When his intentions became known, he would be facing trouble and plenty of it. When they discovered that he had actually moved in and taken possession of the best water in the valley, they would have no choice but to buy him out, run him out, or kill him. Or they could move out themselves, and neither Walt Pogue nor Chalk Reynolds was the man for that.

In their fight Ross had no plan to take sides. He was a not too innocent bystander as far as they were concerned. When Bob and Sherry Vernon were considered, he wasn't too sure. He scowled, realizing suddenly that sentiment had no place in such dealings as his. Until he saw Sherry Vernon, he had been a free agent, and now, for better or worse, he was no longer quite so free.

He could not now move with such cold indifference to the tides of war in the Ruby Hills. Now he had an interest, and his strength was lowered to just the degree of that interest. He was fully aware of the fact. It nettled him even as it amused him, for he was always conscious of himself, and viewed his motives with a certain wry, ironic humor, seeing himself always with much more clarity than others saw him.

Yet, despite that, something had been accomplished. He had staked his claim at Thousand Springs, and started his cabin. He had talked with Scott, and won an ally there, for he knew the old man was with him, at least to a point. He had met and measured Walt Pogue, and he knew that Emmett Chubb was now with Reynolds. That would take some investigation, for from all he had learned he had been sure that Pogue had hired Chubb to kill Vin Carter, but now Chubb worked for Reynolds.

Well, the alliance of such men was tied to a dollar sign, and their loyalty was no longer than their next pay day. And there might have been trouble between Pogue and Chubb, and that might be the reason Pogue was so eager to have him killed.

He directed his thoughts toward the Vernons. Bob was all man. Whatever Reynolds and Pogue planned for him, he would not take. He would have his own ideas, and he was a fighter.

What of the other hands who Scott implied were loyal to Levitt rather than Vernon? These men he must consider, too, and must plan carefully for them, for in such an action as he planned, he must be aware of all the conflicting elements in the valley.

The big man in the white hat he had placed at once. Carter had mentioned him with uncertainty, for when Carter left the valley Star Levitt had just arrived and was an unknown quantity.

With that instinctive awareness that the widely experienced man has for such things, Ross Haney knew that he and Star Levitt were slated to be enemies. They were two men who simply could not be friends, for there was a definite clash of personalities and character that made a physical clash inevitable. And Haney was fully aware that Star Levitt was not the soft touch some might believe. He was a dangerous man, a very dangerous man.

IV

Ross Haney found the Cattleman's Rest Hotel was a long building with thirty rooms, a large empty lobby, and off to one side a restaurant. Feeling suddenly hungry, he turned to the desk for a room, his eyes straying toward the restaurant door.

When Haney dropped his war bag, a young man standing in the doorway turned and walked to the desk. "Room?" He smiled as he spoke, and his face was pleasant.

"The best you've got." Ross grinned at him.

The clerk grinned back. "Sorry, but they are all equally bad, even if reasonably clean. Take Fifteen at the end of the hall. You'll be closer to the well."

"Pump?"

The clerk chuckled. "What do you think this is? New York? It's a rope and bucket well. It's been almost a year since we hauled a dead man out of it. The water should be good by now."

"Sure." Ross studied him for a moment. "Where you from? New York?"

"Yes, and Philadelphia, Boston, Richmond, London, and San Francisco, and now . . . Soledad."

"You've been around." Ross rolled a smoke and dropped the sack on the desk for the clerk. "How's the food?"

"Good. Very good . . . and the prettiest waitress west of the Mississippi."

Ross smiled. "Well, if she's like the other girls around here, she's probably a staked claim. I had a big *hombre* with a white hat tell me tonight that one girl was staked out for him."

The clerk looked at him quickly, shrewdly. "Star Levitt?"

"I guess."

"If he meant the lady you had the race with today, I'd say he was doing more hoping than otherwise. Sherry Vernon"—the clerk spoke carefully—"is not an easy claim to stake."

Ross pulled the register around, hesitated an instant, and then wrote his name: *Ross Haney, El Paso*.

The clerk glanced at it, then looked up. "Glad to meet you, Ross. My name is Allan Kinney." He looked down at the name again. "Ross Haney. I've heard that name from somewhere. It's funny," he added musingly, "about a name and a town. Ross Haney, from El Paso. Now you might not be from El Paso at all. You might be from Del Río or Sanderson or Uvalde. You might even be from Cheyenne or from Fort Sumner or White Oaks. What happened to you in El Paso? Or wherever you came from? And why did you come here? Men drift without reason sometimes, but usually there is something. Sometimes the law is behind them, or an outlaw ahead of them. Sometimes they just want new horizons or a change of scene, and sometimes they are hunting for something. You, now, I'd say you had come to Soledad for a reason . . . a reason that could mean trouble."

"Let's drink some coffee," Haney suggested, "and see if that waitress is as pretty as you say."

"You won't think so," Kinney said, shaking his head, "you won't think so at all. You've just seen Sherry Vernon. After her all women looked washed out . . . until you get over her."

"I don't plan on it."

The two men entered the restaurant and selected a table. Kinney dropped into a chair. "That, my friend, is a large order. Miss Vernon usually handles such situations with neatness and dispatch. She is always pleasant, never familiar."

"This is different." Ross, seated now, looked up and suddenly he knew with a queer excitement just what he was going to say. He said it. "I'm going to marry her."

Allan Kinney gulped. "Have you told her? Does she know your intentions are honorable? Does she even know you have intentions?" He grinned. "You know, friend, that is a large order you have laid out for yourself."

The waitress came up. She was a slender, very pretty girl with red hair, a few freckles, and a sort of bubbling good humor that was contagious.

"May," Kinney said, "I want you to meet Ross Haney. He is going to marry Sherry Vernon."

At this Ross felt his ears getting red and cursed himself for a thick-headed fool for ever saying such a thing. It may have been startled from him by the sudden realization that he intended to do just that.

"What?" May said quickly, looking at him, "another one?"

Haney glanced up and suddenly he put his hand over hers and said gently: "No, May. *The* one!"

Her eyes held his for a moment, and the laughter faded from them. "You know," she said seriously, "I think you might!"

She went for their coffee. Kinney looked at Ross with care. "Friend Haney," he said, "you have made an impression. I really think the lady believed you. Now if you can do as well with Miss Vernon, you'll be doing all right."

The door opened suddenly from the street and two men stepped in. Ross glanced up, and his dark eyes held on the two men who stood there. One of the men was a big man with sloping shoulders, and his eyes caught Haney's and narrowed as if in sudden recognition. The other man was shorter, thicker, but obviously a hardcase. Ross guessed that these men were from the Vernon ranch—or they could be, riders at least who knew about Ross Haney and were more than casually interested. These could be the men who worked for Star Levitt, and as such they merited study, yet their type was not an unfamiliar one to Ross Haney, or to any man who rode the borderlands or the wild country. While many a cowpuncher has branded a few mavericks or rustled a few cows when he needed drinking money, or wanted a new saddle, there was a certain intangible, yet very real difference that marked those who held to the outlaw trail, and both of these men had it. They were men with guns for hire, men who rode for trouble, and for the ready cash they could get for crooked work. He knew their type. He had faced such men before, and he knew they recognized him. These men were a type who never fought a battle for anyone but themselves.

No sooner were these two seated than May brought their coffee. Then, without warning, the door pushed open again and two more men came into the room. Ross glanced around and caught the eye of a short, stocky man who walked with a quick, jerky lift of his knees. He walked now— right over to Haney.

"You're Ross Haney?" he said abruptly. "I've got a job for you! Start tomorrow morning! A hundred a month an' found. Plenty of horses! I'm Chalk Reynolds an' my place is just out of town in that big clump of cottonwoods. Old place. You won't have any trouble finding it."

Ross smiled. "Sorry, I'm not hunting a job."

Reynolds had been turning away; he whipped back quickly. "What do you mean? Not looking for a job? At a hundred a month? When the range is covered with top hands gettin' forty?"

"I said I didn't want a job."

"Ah?" The genial light left the older man's face, and his blue eyes hardened and narrowed. "So that's it! You've gone to work for Walt Pogue!"

"No, I don't work for Pogue. I don't work for anybody. I'm my own man, Mister Reynolds."

Chalk Reynolds stared at him. "Listen, my friend, and listen well. In the Ruby Hills today there are but two factions, those for Reynolds, and those against him. If you don't work for me, I'll regard you as an enemy."

Haney shrugged. "That's your funeral. From all I hear you have enemies enough without choosing any more. Also, from all I hear, you deserve them."

"What?" Reynolds's eyes blazed. "Don't sass me, stranger!"

The lean, whip-bodied man beside him touched his arm. "Let me handle this, Uncle Chalk," he said gently. "Let me talk to this man."

Ross shifted his eyes. The younger man had a lantern jaw and unusually long gray eyes. The eyes had a flatness about them that puzzled and warned him. "My name is Sydney Berdue. I am foreman for Mister Reynolds." He stepped closer to where Haney sat in his chair, one elbow on the table. "Maybe you would like to tell me why he deserves his enemies."

Haney glanced up at him, his blunt features composed, faintly curious, his eyes steady and aware. "Sure," he said quietly. "I'd be glad to. Chalk Reynolds came West from Missouri right after the war with Mexico. For a time he was located in Santa Fé, but, as the wagon trains started to come West, he went north and began selling guns to the Indians."

Reynolds's face went white and his eyes blazed. "That's not true!"

Haney's glance cut his words short. "Don't make me kill you," Ross said sharply. "Every word I say is true. You took part in wagon train raids yourself. I expect you collected your portion of white scalps. Then you got out of there with a good deal of loot and met a man in Julesburg who wanted to come out here. He knew nothing of your crooked background, and. . . ."

Berdue's hand was a streak for his gun, but Haney had expected it. When the Reynolds foreman stepped toward him, he had come beyond Haney's outstretched feet, and Ross whipped his toe up behind the foreman's knee and jerked hard just as he shoved with his open hand. Berdue hit the floor with a crash and his gun went off with a roar, the shot plowing into the ceiling. From the room overhead came an angry shout and the sound of bare feet hitting the floor.

Ross moved swiftly. He stepped over and kicked the gun from Berdue's hand, then swept it up.

"Get up! Reynolds, get over there against the wall, *pronto!*"

White-faced, Reynolds backed to the wall, hatred burning deeply in his eyes. Slowly Sydney Berdue got to his feet, his eyes clinging to his gun in Ross Haney's hand.

"Lift your hands, both of you. Now push them higher. Hold it."

He stared at the two men. Behind him, the room was silent with curious onlookers. "Now," Ross Haney said coolly, "I'm going to finish what I started. You asked me why you deserved to have enemies. I started by telling you about the white people you murdered, and by the guns you sold, and now I'll tell you about the man you met in Julesburg."

Reynolds's face was ashen. "Forget that," he said. "You don't need to talk so much. Berdue was huntin' trouble. You forget it. I need a good man."

"To murder . . . like you did your partner? You

70

made a deal with him, and he came down here and worked hard. He planted those trees. He built that house. Then three of you went out and stumbled into a band of Indians, and somehow, although wounded, you were the only one who got back. And naturally the ranch was all yours. Who were those Indians, Chalk? Or was there only *one* Indian? Only one, who was the last man of three riding single file? You wanted to know why I wouldn't work for you and why you should have enemies. I've told you. And now I'll tell you something more. I've come to the Ruby Hills to stay. I'm not leavin'."

Delibcrately he handed the gun back to Berdue, and, as he held it out to him, their eyes met and fastened, and it was Sydney Berdue's eyes that shifted first. He took the gun, reversed it, and started it into his holster, and then his hand stopped and his lips drew tight.

Ross Haney was smiling. "Careful, Berdue," he said softly. "I wouldn't try it, if I were you."

Berdue stared, and then with an oath he shoved the gun hard into its holster and, turning out the door, walked rapidly away. Behind him went Chalk Reynolds, his neck and ears red with the bitterness of the fury that throbbed in his veins.

Slowly, in a babble of talk, Ross Haney seated himself again. "May," he called over to the waitress, "my coffee's cold! Bring me another one, will you?"

V

Persons who lived in the town of Soledad were not unaccustomed to sensation, but the calling of Chalk Reynolds and his supposedly gun-slick foreman in the Cattleman's Rest Hotel restaurant was a subject that had the old maids of both sexes licking their lips with anticipation and excitement. Little had been known of the background of Chalk Reynolds. He was the oldest settler, the owner of the biggest and oldest ranch, and he was a hard character when pushed. Yet now they saw him in a new light, and the story went from mouth to mouth.

Not the last to hear it was Walt Pogue, who chuckled and slapped his heavy thigh. "Wouldn't you know it? That old four-flusher! Crooked as a dog's hind leg!"

The next thing that occurred to anyone occurred to him. How did Ross Haney know? The thought brought Pogue to a standstill. Haney knew too much. Who was Haney? If he knew that, he might . . . but, no! That didn't necessarily follow. Still, Ross Haney would be a good friend to have, or a bad enemy.

Not the least of the talk concerned Haney's confidence, the way he had stood there and dared Berdue to draw. Overnight Haney had become the most talked-about man in the Ruby Hills.

When gathering his information about the Ruby Hills country, Ross Haney had gleaned some other information that was of great interest. That information was what occupied his mind on his second day in Soledad.

So far, in his meandering around the country, and he had done more of it than anyone believed, he had had no opportunity to verify this final fragment of information. But now he intended to do it. From what he had overheard, the country north and west of the mountains was a badlands that was avoided by all. It was a lava country, broken and jagged, and there was much evidence of prehistoric volcanic action, so much so that riding there was a danger always, and walking was the surest way to ruin a pair of boots.

Yet at one time there had been a man who knew the lava beds and all of that badlands country that occupied some 300 square miles stretching north and west across the state line. That man had been Jim Burge.

It had been Jim Burge who had told Charlie Hastings, Reynolds's ill-fated partner, about the Ruby Hills country, and it had been Jim Burge who first drove a herd of Spanish cattle into the Ruby Hills. But Burge tired of ranching and headed north, leaving his ranch and turning his horses loose. His cattle were already gone. Gone, that is, into the badlands. Burge knew where they were, but cattle were of no use without a market, and there was no market anywhere near. Burge decided he wanted to move, and he wanted quick money, so he left the country, taking only a few of the best horses with him.

He had talked to Charlie Hastings and Hastings had talked to Chalk Reynolds, but Jim Burge was already gone. Gone east into the Texas Panhandle and a lone-hand fight with Comanches that ended with four warriors dead and with Jim Burge's scalp hanging from the belt of another. But Jim Burge had talked to other people in Santa Fé, and the others did not forget, either. One of these had talked to Ross Haney, and Ross was a curious man.

When he threw his saddle on the Appaloosa, he was planning to satisfy that curiosity. He was going to find out what had become of those cattle. Nine years had passed since Burge left them to shift for themselves. In nine years several hundred cattle can do pretty well for themselves.

"There's water in those badlands if you know where to look," Burge had told the man in Santa Fé, "an' there's grass, but you've got to find it." Knowing range cattle, Ross was not worried about the cattle finding it, and, if they could find it, he would find them—unless someone else had.

So he rode out of Soledad down the main trail, and there were many eyes that followed him out.

One pair of these belonged to Sherry Vernon, already out and on her horse, drifting over the range, inspecting her cattle and seeing where they fed. She noted the tall rider on the queerly marked horse, and there was a strange leap in her heart as she watched him heading down the trail.

Was he leaving? For always? The thought gave her a pang, even though, remembering the oddly intent look in his eyes and the hard set to his jaw, she knew he would be back. Of course, she had heard the story of his meeting with Chalk Reynolds and Sydney Berdue. Berdue had always frightened her, for wherever she turned, his eyes were upon her. They gave her a crawling sensation, not at all like the excitement she drew from the quick, amused eyes of Ross Haney.

The Appaloosa was a good mountain horse, and, ears pricked forward, he stepped out eagerly. The sights and smells were what he knew best and he quickened his step, sure he was going home. Ross Haney knew that with his action of the previous day he was in the center of things whether he liked it or not, and he liked it. From now on he would move fast, and with boldness, not too definitely, for it would pay to keep them puzzled for a few days longer. Things would break shortly between Pogue and Reynolds, especially now that his needling of Reynolds would scare the old man into aggressive action.

Chalk was no fool. He would know how fast talk would spread. It might not be long before embarrassing questions might be asked. The only escape from those questions lay in power. He must put himself beyond questions. Eyes squinted against the glare, Haney thought about that, trying to calculate just what Reynolds would do. It was up to him to strike, and he would strike, or Haney knew nothing of men under pressure.

The trail he sought showed itself suddenly, just a faint track off to the right through the piñons, and he took it, letting Río set his own gait. It was mid-afternoon before Ross reached the edge of the lava beds. The black tumbled masses seemed without trails or any sign of vegetation. He skirted the great black, tumbled masses of lava, searching for some evidence of a trail. It was miserably hot, and the sun threw heat back from the blazing rocks until he felt like he was in an oven. When he was on a direct line between the lava beds and Thousand Springs, he rode back up the mountain, halted, and swung down to give his horse a rest.

From his saddlebags he took a telescope, a glass he had bought in New Orleans several years before. Sitting down on a boulder while the Appaloosa cropped casually at the dry grass, he began a systematic, inch by inch study of the lava beds.

Only the vaguest sort of plan had formed in his mind for his next step. Everything had been worked out carefully to this point, but from now on his action depended much upon the actions of Pogue and Reynolds. Yet he did have the vestige of a plan. If the cattle he sought were still in the lava beds, he intended to brand them one by one and shove bunches of them out into the valley. He was going to use that method to make his bid for the valley range.

After a half hour of careful study he got up, thrust the glass in his belt, and rode slowly along the hillside, stopping at intervals to continue his examination of the beds. It was almost dusk when he raised up in the stirrups and pointed the glass toward a tall finger of rock that thrust itself high from the beds. At the base of it was a cow, and it was walking slowly toward the northwest!

Try as he might, Ross could find no trail into the lava beds, so as dusk was near, he turned the Appaloosa and started back toward Thousand Springs. He would try again. At least, he knew he was not shooting in the dark. There was at least one cow in that labyrinth of lava, and, if there was one, there would certainly be more.

The trail he had chosen led him up the mesa at Thousand Springs from a little known route. He wound around through the clumps of piñon until the flat top was reached. Then he rode along slowly, drinking in this beauty that he had chosen for the site of his home. The purple haze had thickened over the hills and darkened among the trees, and deep shadows gathered in the forested notches of the hills while the pines yet made a dark fringe against the sky still red with the last rose of the sinking sun.

Below him, the mesa broke sharply off and fell for over 100 feet of sheer rock. Thirty feet from the bottom of the cliff the springs trickled from the fractured rock and covered the rock below with a silver sheen from many small cascades that fell away into the pool below.

Beyond the far edge of the pool, fringed with aspens, the valley fell away in a long sweep of tall-grass range, rolling into a dark distance against the mystery of the hills. Ross Haney sat his horse in a place rarely seen by man, for he was doubtful if anyone in many years had mounted the mesa. That he was not the first man here, he knew, for there were Indian relics and the remains of stone houses, ages old. These seemed to have no connection with any cliff dwellings or pueblos he had seen in the past. The building was more ancient and more massive than on Acoma, the Sky City.

The range below him was the upper end of Ruby Valley and was supposedly under control of Chalk Reynolds. Actually Reynolds rarely visited the place, nor did his men. It was far away at the end of the range he claimed, and the water was available for the cattle when they wished to come to it. Yet here on the rim of the mesa, or slightly back from the rim, Haney had begun to build a ranch house, using the old foundations of the prehistoric builders, and many of their stones.

The floor itself was intact, and he availed himself of it, sweeping it clean over a wide expanse. He had paced it off, and planned his house accordingly, and he had large ideas. Yet for the moment he was intent only on repairing a part of the house to use as his claim shanty.

There was water here. It bubbled from the same source as that of the Thousand Springs. He knew that his water was the same water. Several times he had tried dropping sticks or leaves into the water outside his door, only to find them later in the pool below.

From where he sat he could with his glass see several miles of trail, and watch all who approached him. The trail up the back way was unknown so far as he could find out. Certainly it indicated no signs of use but that of wild game, although it had evidently been used in bygone years.

To the east and south his view was unobstructed. Below him lay all the dark distance of the valley and the range for which he was fighting. To the north, the mesa broke off sharply and fell away into a deep cañon with a dry wash at its bottom. The side of the cañon across from him was almost as sheer as this and at least a quarter of a mile away.

The trail led up from the west and through a broken country of tumbled rock, long fingers of lava, and clumps of piñon giving way to aspen and pine. The top of the mesa was at least 200 acres in extent and absolutely impossible to reach by any known route but the approach he used.

Returning through the trees to a secluded hollow, Ross swung down and stripped the saddle and bridle from the Appaloosa, then turned it loose. He rarely hobbled or tied the horse, for Río would come at a call or whistle, and never failed to respond at once. But a horse in most cases will not wander far from a camp-fire, feeding away from it, and then slowly feeding back toward it, seeming to like the feeling of comfort as well as a man did.

He built his fire of dry wood and built it with plenty of cover, keeping it small. Even at this height there was no danger of it being seen and causing wonder. The last thing he wanted now was for any of the people from the valley to find him out.

After he had eaten, he strolled back to the open ground where the house was taking shape. Part of the ancient rock floor he was keeping for a ter-race from which the whole valley could be seen.

For a long time he stood there, looking off into the darkness and enjoying the cool night air. Then he turned and walked back into the deep shadows of the house. He was standing there, trying to see it as it would appear when complete when he heard a low, distant rumble.

Suddenly anxious, he listened intently. It seemed to come from within the very rock on which he stood. He waited, listening for the sound to grow. But after a moment it died away to a vague rumble, and then disappeared altogether. Puzzled, he walked around for several minutes, waiting and listening, but there was no further sound.

It was a strange thing, and it disturbed him and left him uneasy as he walked back to his camp. Long after he rolled in his blankets, he lay there puzzling over it. He noted with an odd sense of disquiet that Río stayed close to him, closer than usual. Of course, there could be another reason for that. There were cougars on the mesa and in the breaks behind it. He had seen their tracks. There were also elk and deer, and twice he had seen bear. The country he had chosen was wildly beautiful, a strange, lost corner of the land, somehow cut off from the valley by the rampart of Thousand Springs Mesa.

Ross Haney awakened suddenly as the sky was growing gray, and found himself sitting bolt upright. And then he heard it again, that low, mounting rumble, far down in the rock beneath him, as though the very spirit of the mountain had been rolling over under him in his sleep. Only here the sound was not so plain, it was fainter, farther away.

VI

At daybreak, Ross rolled out of his blankets, built a fire, and made coffee. While eating, he puzzled over the strange sound he had heard the night before and again before dawn. The only solution that seemed logical was that it came somehow from the springs. It was obvious that forces of some sort were at work deep in the rock of the mesa.

Obviously these forces had made no recent change in the contour of the rock itself, and so must be insufficient for the purpose. Haney continued with his building, working the morning through.

Unlike many cowhands, he had always enjoyed working with his hands. Now he had the pleasure of doing something for himself, with the feeling that he was building to last. By noon he had another wall of heavy stone constructed and the house was beginning to take shape.

He stopped briefly to eat, and slipped on his shirt before sitting down. As he buttoned it up, he saw a faint movement far down the Soledad trail. Going to his saddlebags, he dug out his glass and took his position in a lookout post among the rocks on the rim. First making sure the sunlight would not reflect from the glass and give him away, he dropped flat among the rocks and pointed the glass downtrail.

The rider's face was still indistinct, but there was something vaguely familiar about him. And then, as he drew nearer, Ross saw it was Sydney Berdue.

What was the Reynolds foreman doing here? Of course, as this was considered RR range, he might be checking the grass or the stock. He rode swiftly, however, and paid no attention to anything around him. When he reached the pool below, he swung down, seated himself on a rock, and lighted a cigarette.

Waiting for someone.

The sun felt warm and comfortable on Ross's back after the hard work of the morning and he settled himself comfortably into the warm sand behind the rocks. Thoughtfully he turned his glass down the trail, but saw no one else. Then he began scanning the country and, after a few minutes, picked up another rider. The man rode a sorrel horse with three white stockings and must have approached through the timber as he was not in sight until the last minute. He rode swiftly up to the pool and swung down. The two men shook hands, and, puzzled, Ross shifted his glass to the brand.

The sorrel carried a VV on his shoulder! A Vernon rider at what was apparently a secret meeting with the foreman of the RR! The two seated themselves, and Haney waited, studying them, and then the trail. And now he saw two more horsemen, and these were riding up the trail together. One was a big, slope-shouldered man who he had seen in Soledad, and he rode a Box N horse. The last man rode a gray mustang with the Three Diamonds of Star Levitt on his hip.

Here was something of real interest. The four brands, two of them outwardly at war, the others on the verge of it, meeting in secret. Haney cursed his luck that he could not hear what was said, but so far as he could see, Berdue seemed to be laying down the law.

Then he saw something else.

At first it was a vague suggestion of disturbance in the grass and brush near the foot of the cliff, and then he saw a slight figure, creeping nearer. His heart leaped as he saw Sherry Vernon crawling nearer. Sherry Vernon!

Whatever the meeting of the four men meant, it was at least plain that they intended no one to see or overhear what they had to say. If the girl was seen or heard, she would be in great danger. Sliding back from his lookout point, he hurried in a crouching run toward the house and got his Winchester.

By the time he was back, the brief meeting was breaking up. The girl lay still below him, and the men mounted, one by one, and rode away. The last to go was Sydney Berdue.

After several minutes had passed, Sherry got to her feet and walked out in the open. She went to the spring and drank, then stood looking around, obviously in profound thought.

Ross debated the possibility of getting his horse, but dismissed it as impossible. It would require a couple of hours at least to ride from here to the spring, although he was within a few hundred feet of it.

The girl walked away toward the woods, finally, evidently going for her horse. After some minutes she rode out of the trees on Flame and started down the trail toward the VV Ranch, distant against the far hills.

There had been a meeting of the four brands, but not of the leaders. Sherry Vernon had probably overheard what was said. He scowled thoughtfully. The girl had moved with care and skill, and her actions showed she was no mean woodsman when it came to playing the Indian. None of the four below had been a tenderfoot, yet she had approached them and listened without giving herself away. Sherry Vernon, he decided, would bear some watching herself.

Saddling Río, Ross rode back through the aspens and down the lonely and dangerous trail to the rim of the badlands. He still had found no way to enter the lava beds, and, if he was to take the next step in his program of conquest, he must find the cattle that he was sure still roamed among those remote and lost water holes in the lava.

The afternoon was well along before he found himself skirting the rim of the cañon that opened near the lava beds, and, when he reached them, it was already late. There would be little time for a search, but, despite that, he turned north, planning to cut back around the mesa and return to Soledad by way of the springs.

A slight movement among the trees ahead caused him to halt, and then he saw several elk drifting slowly down a narrow glade toward the lava. His eyes narrowed suddenly. There was no water of which he knew closer than the Thousand Springs pool, and these elk were drifting away from it rather than toward it. As they usually watered at sundown or before daybreak, they must be headed for water elsewhere, and that could be in the lava.

Dismounting, he ground-hitched his horse and watched the elk as they drifted along until they had almost vanished in the trees, then he mounted and followed them down. When the trail he was following turned down and joined theirs, he continued along it. In a few minutes he grunted with satisfaction, for the hoof marks led him right up to the lava and into a narrow cleft between two great folds of the black rocks.

Riding carefully, for the trail was very narrow and the lava on both sides black and rough, he kept on, following the elk. It was easy to see how such a trail might exist for years and never be found, for at times he was forced to draw one leg up and lift the stirrup out of the way, as it was too narrow, otherwise.

The trail wound around and around, covering much distance without penetrating very far, and then it dipped down suddenly through a jagged and dangerous-looking cleft. Ross hesitated, studying the loose-hanging crags above with misgiving. They looked too shaky and insecure for comfort. He well knew that if a man was ever trapped or hurt in this lava bed, he might as well give up. There would be no help for him. Yet, with many an upward glance at the great, poorly balanced chunks of rock, many of them weighing many tons, he rode down into the cleft on the trail of the elk.

For over a half mile the cleft led him steadily downward, much of the going very steep, and he realized that he was soon going to be well below the level of the surrounding country. He rode on, however, despite the growing darkness, already great in the dark bottom of the cleft. Then the trail opened out, and he stopped with a gasp of amazement.

Before him lay a great circular valley, an enormous valley surrounded by gigantic black cliffs that in many places shelved out over the edge, but the bottom was almost level and was covered with rich green grass. There were a few scattered clumps of trees, and from somewhere he heard the sound of water.

Drifting on, he looked up and around him, overcome with astonishment. The depth of the valley, at least 1,000 feet lower than the surrounding country, and the unending sameness of the view of the beds from above safely concealed its existence. It was without doubt an ancient volcanic crater, long extinct, and probably the source of the miles of lava beds that had been spewed forth in some bygone age.

The green fields below were dotted with cattle, most of them seemingly in excellent shape. Here and there among them he noticed small groups of horses. Without doubt these were the cattle and horses, or their descendants, left by Jim Burge.

Despite the lateness of the hour, he pushed on, marveling at the mighty walls around him, at the green grass, and the white-trunked aspens. Twice he found springs of water; in both cases they bubbled from the ground. Later, he found one spring that ran from a cleft in the rock and trickled down over the worn face of the cliff for some thirty feet to sink into the ground below. None of the cattle seemed in the least frightened of him, although they moved back as he approached, and several lifted their noses at him curiously.

When he had ridden for well over two miles, he drew up in a small glade near a spring, and, stripping the saddle from his horse, he made camp. This would end his rations, and tomorrow he must start back. Obviously this would be a good place to start such a cache of supplies as Scott had advised.

Night brought a strange coolness to the valley. He built a fire and fixed his coffee, talking to Río meanwhile. After a moment he became conscious of movement. He looked up and saw that a dozen or more cows and a bull had moved up. They were staring at him with their amazed bovine eyes. Apparently they had never seen a man before.

From all appearances, the crater was a large one, being several miles across and carpeted with this rich grass. The cattle were all in good shape. Twice during the night he heard the cry of a cougar and once the howl of a wolf.

With daylight he was in saddle once more, but by day the crater proved to be smaller than he had at first believed, and there was probably some 2,000 acres in the bottom. But it was all the same level ground with rich grass and a good bit of timber, all things considered.

Twice, when skirting the edges of the crater, he found ice caves. These he knew were caused by the mass cooling so unevenly that, when the surface had become cold and hard, the material below was still molten. As the fluid drained away, caves were formed under the solid crust. Because lava is a poor heat conductor, the cold air of the caves was protected. Ice formed there, and no matter how warm it might be on the surface, there was always snow in the caves. At places pools of clear, cold water had formed. He could see that some of these had been used as watering places by the deer, elk, and wild horses.

When at last he started back toward the cleft through which he had gained entrance to the crater, he was sure there were several hundred, perhaps as many as 600 head of wild cattle in the bottom of the crater.

He rode out, but not with any feeling of comfort. Someday he would scale those cliffs and have a look at the craggy boulders on the rim. If someone ever fell into the cleft, whoever or whatever was in the bottom would never come out.

It was dusk of another evening before the Appaloosa cantered down the one street of Soledad and drew up at the livery stable. A Mexican came to the door, glanced at him, and then accepted his horse. He looked doubtfully at the strange brand.

"You ride for *Señor* Pogue or *Señor* Reynolds?" he asked hesitantly.

"For myself," Ross said. "What's the matter? The town seems quiet."

"*Sí, señor*. There has been a keeling. Rolly Burt of the RR was in a shooting with two hands from the Box N. One of them was killed, the other wounded, and *Señor* Burt has disappeared."

"Left the country?"

"Who knows? He was wounded, they say, and I am sorry for that. He was a good man, *Señor* Burt." The Mexican lighted a smoke, glancing at Haney. "Perhaps he was no longer wanted on the RR, either."

"Why do you say that?" Ross asked quickly. "Have you any reason for it?"

"*Sí*. He has told me himself that he has trouble weeth *Señor* Berdue."

Berdue had trouble with Burt, yet Burt was attacked by two Box N hands? That didn't seem to tie in, or did it? Could there be any connection between this shooting and the meeting at the springs? In any event, this would probably serve to start hostilities again.

VII

Leaving his horse to be cared for, Ross returned to his room in the Cattleman's Rest Hotel. Kinney was not in the lobby when he crossed it, and he found no one on the stairs. He knew how precarious was his own position, for while the house he was building was reasonably safe from discovery, there was no reason to believe that someone would not soon discover the ground had been plowed back under the trees. It wasn't much, but enough to indicate he was working on the place.

Uneasily he surveyed the situation. So far everything was proceeding according to plan, and almost too well. He had his water rights under control. He had found the cattle. He had in the crater and on the mesa two bases of action that were reasonably safe from attack, yet the situation was due to blow up at almost any moment.

Berdue seemed to be playing a deep game. It might be with the connivance of his uncle, but he might be on his own. Perhaps someone else had the same idea he had, that from the fighting of Pogue and Reynolds would come a new system of things in the Ruby Hills country. Perhaps Berdue, or some other unnamed person or group, planned to be top dog.

Berdue's part in it puzzled Haney, but at least

he knew by sight the men Berdue had met secretly and would be able to keep a closer watch on them. Also, there were still the strange hardcases who lived and worked on the VV. Somehow they did not seem to fit with what he had seen of the Vernons. *The next order of business,* he told himself, *is a visit to the VV.*

A dozen people were eating in the hotel restaurant when he entered. He stopped at one side of the door and surveyed the groups with care. It would not do to walk into Berdue or Reynolds unawares, for Berdue would not, and Reynolds dared not, ignore him. He had stepped into the scene in Soledad in no uncertain terms.

Suddenly, at a small table alone, he saw Sherry Vernon. On an impulse, he walked over to her, his spurs jingling. She glanced up at him, momentarily surprised.

"Oh, it's you again? I thought you had left town."

"You know better than that." He indicated the chair opposite her. "May I sit down?"

"Surely." She looked at him thoughtfully. "You know, Ross Haney, you're not an entirely unhandsome sort of man, but I've a feeling you're still pretty savage."

"I live in a country that is savage," he said simply. "It is a country that is untamed. The last court of appeal is a six-shooter."

"From all I hear, you gave Sydney Berdue some

uncomfortable moments without one. You're quite an unusual man. Sometimes your language sounds like any cowboy, and sometimes it doesn't, and sometimes your ideas are different."

"You find men of all kinds in the West. The town drunk in Julesburg, when I was there, could quote Shakespeare and had two degrees. I punched cows on the range in Texas with the brother of an English lord."

"Are you suggesting that you are a duke in disguise?"

"Me?" He grinned. "No, I'm pretty much what I seem. I'm a cowhand, a drifter. Only I've got a few ideas and I've read a few books. I spent a winter once snowed up in the mountains in Montana with two other cowhands. All we had for entertainment was a couple of decks of cards, some checkers, and a half dozen books. Some Englishman left them there, and I expect before spring we all knew those books by heart, an' we'd argued every point in them."

"What were they?" she asked curiously.

"Plutarch's LIVES, the plays and sonnets of Shakespeare, some history . . . oh, a lot of stuff. And good reading. We had a lot of fun with those books. When we'd played cards and checkers until we were black in the face, we'd ask each other questions on the books, for by the time we'd been there half the winter we'd read them several times over."

He ate in silence for a few minutes, and then she asked: "Do you know anything about the shooting?"

"Heard about it. What sort of man is Rolly Burt?"

"One of the best. You'd like him, I think. Hard as nails, and no youngster. He's more than forty, I'd say. But he says what he thinks, and he thinks a good deal."

Ross hesitated a few minutes, and then said: "By the way, I saw one of your hands in town yesterday. A tall, slope-shouldered fellow in a checkered shirt. You know the one I mean?"

She looked up at him, her eyes cool and direct. He had an uncomfortable feeling that she knew more than she was allowing him to think she did. Of course, this was the man she had watched from hiding as he met Berdue. Probably she had overheard their talk.

"Oh, you mean Kerb Dahl! Yes, he's one of our hands. Why do you ask?"

"Wondering about him. I'm trying to get folks placed around here."

"There are a lot of them trying to get you placed, too."

He laughed. "Sure! I expected that. Are you one of them?"

"Yes, I think I am. You remember I overheard your talk on the trail and I'm still wondering where you plan to be top dog?"

He flushed. "You shouldn't have heard that. However, I back down on none of it. I know how Chalk Reynolds got his ranch. I know how Walt Pogue got his, and neither of them has any moral nor other claim to them aside from possession, if that is a right. You probably heard what I told Chalk in here the other day. I could tell him more. I haven't started on Pogue yet, and I'd as soon you didn't tell anyone I plan to. However, in good time I shall. You see, he ran old man Carter off his place, and he had Emmett Chubb kill Vin Carter. That's one of the things that drew me here."

"Revenge?"

"Call it what you like. I have a different name for it." He leaned toward her, suddenly eager for her to understand. "You see, you can't judge the West by any ordered land you know. It is a wild, hard land, and the men that came West and survived were tough stern men. They fought Indians and white men who were worse than Indians. They fought winter, flood, storm, drought, and starvation. There's a sheriff here in town who was practically appointed by Chalk Reynolds. The jail here stands on Reynolds's land. The nearest court is over two hundred miles away, over poor roads and through Indian country. North of us there is one of the wildest and most remote lands in North America where a criminal could escape and hide for years. The only law we

96

have here is the law of strength. The only justice we have must live in the hearts and minds of men. The land is hard, and so the men are hard. We make mistakes, of course, but when there is a case of murder, we try to handle the murderer so he will not kill again. Someday we will have law. We will have order. Then we can let the courts decide, but now we have none of those things. If we find a mad dog, we kill him, for there is no dogcatcher or law to do it. If we find a man who kills unfairly, we punish him. If two men fight and all is equal, regardless of which cause is right, we let the killing stand. But if a man is shot in the back, without a gun or a fair chance, then the people or sometimes one man must act.

"I agree that it is not right. I agree that it should be different, but this is yet a raw, hard land, and we must have our killers, not punished, but prevented from killing again. Vin Carter was my friend. Of that I can say nothing, only that because he was my friend, I must act for him. He was not a gunfighter. He was a brave young man, a fair shot, and, on the night he was killed, he was so drunk he could scarcely see. He did not even know what was happening. It was murder.

"So I have come here. It so happens that I am like some of these men. Perhaps I am ruthless. Perhaps in the long run I shall lose, and perhaps I shall gain. No man is perfect. No man is altogether right or altogether wrong. Pogue and Reynolds got their ranches and power through violence. They are now in a dog-eat-dog feud of their own. When that war is over, I expect to have a good ranch. If it leaves them both alive and in power, I shall have my ranch, anyway."

She looked at him thoughtfully. "Where, Ross?"

His pulse leaped at the use of his first name, and he smiled suddenly. "Does it matter now? Let's wait, and then I'll tell you." The smile left his face. "By the way, as you left me the other day, a man told me you were a staked claim, and to stay away."

"What did you do?" She looked at him gravely, curiously.

"I told him he was a fool to believe any woman was a staked claim unless she wanted it so. And he said, nevertheless you were staked. If it is of interest, you might as well know that I don't believe him. Also, I wouldn't pay any attention if I did."

She smiled. "I would be surprised if you did. Nevertheless"—her chin lifted a little—"what he said is true."

Ross Haney's heart seemed to stop. For a full minute he stared at her, amazed and wordless. Then he said: "You mean . . . what?"

"I mean that I'm engaged to marry Star Levitt. I have been engaged to him for three months."

She arose swiftly. "I must be going now." Her hand dropped suddenly to his with a gentle pressure, and then she was gone.

He stared after her. His thoughts refused to order themselves, for of all the things she might have said, or that he might have expected, this was the last. Sherry Vernon was engaged to Star Levitt.

"Some hot coffee?" It was May, smiling down at him.

"Sure." She cleaned up the table, then left him alone. *Sure,* he mused, *that's the way it would be. I meet a girl worth having and she belongs to somebody else!*

"Mind if I sit down?"

He looked up to see Allan Kinney, the hotel clerk, standing by the table. "Go ahead," he suggested, "and have some coffee."

May delivered the coffee, and for a few moments there was silence.

"Ross, you'd do a lot for a friend, wouldn't you?"

Surprised, he glanced up and something in Kinney's eyes told him what was coming. "Why, sure!" But even as he said it, he was thinking it over, thinking over what he knew Kinney had on his mind.

"Do you regard me as a friend? Of course, I haven't known you long, but you seem like a regular fellow. You haven't any local ties that I can see."

"That's right! I just cut the last one. Or had it cut. What do you want me to do? Get him out of town?"

Kinney jerked up sharply. "You mean . . . you know?"

"I guessed. Where else would he go? Is Burt hurt bad?"

"He can ride. He's a good man, Ross. One of the best. I had no idea what to do about him because I know they will think of the hotel soon."

"You've got him here?" Haney was incredulous. "We'd best get him out tonight. That Box N crowd will be in hunting for him, and I've got a hunch the RR outfit won't back him the least bit."

"He's in the potato cellar. In a box under the potatoes."

"Whatever made you ask me?" Ross demanded.

Kinney shrugged. "Well, like I said, you hadn't any ties here, and seemed on the prod, as they say in Soledad. Then, May suggested it. May did, and Sherry."

"She knows?"

"I thought of her first. The VV is out of this fight so far, and it seemed the only place. She told me she would like to, but there were reasons why it was the very worst place for him. Then she suggested you."

"She did?"

"Uhn-huh. She said, if you liked Burt, she knew you would do it, and you might do it just as a slap at Reynolds and Pogue. She didn't seem to believe Reynolds would help, either."

Haney digested this thoughtfully. Apparently Sherry had a pretty good idea of just what undercurrents were moving the pawns about in the Soledad chess game. Of course, she would have heard at least part of Berdue's talk with Kerb Dahl and the others.

"We can't wait," Haney said. "It will have to be done now. The Box N hands should be getting to town within the hour. Have you got a spare horse?"

"Not that we can get without everybody knowing, but May has one at her place," Kinney answered. "She lives on the edge of town. The problem is to get him there."

"I'll get him there," Haney promised. "But I'd best get mounted myself. I know where to take him, too. However, you'd best throw us together a sack of grub from the restaurant supplies so there won't be too many questions asked. After I come back again, I can arrange to get some stuff."

Ross Haney got to his feet. "Get him ready to move. I'll get my horse down to May's and come back." He listened while Kinney gave him directions about finding her house, and then hurried to the door.

It was too late.

A dozen hard-riding horsemen came charging up the street and they swung down at the hotel. One man stepped up on the boardwalk and strode into the hotel. Haney knew him by his size. It was Walt Pogue himself, and the man at his right was the man who had been with Berdue at the springs!

"Kinney! I want to search your place! That killer Rolly Burt is somewhere in town, an' by the Lord Harry we'll have him hangin' from a cottonwood limb before midnight!"

"What makes you think he'd be here?" Kinney demanded. He was pale and taut, but completely self-possessed. He might have been addressing a class in history, or reading a paper before a literary group. "I know Burt, but I haven't seen him."

VIII

Unobtrusively Ross Haney was lounging against the door to the kitchen, his mind working swiftly. They would find Burt, and there was no earthly way to prevent it. The only chance would be to avert the hanging, to delay it. He knew suddenly that he was not going to see Rolly Burt hang. He didn't know the man, but Burt had won his sympathy by winning a fair fight against two men.

"What are you so all fired wrought up about, Pogue?" he drawled.

Walt Pogue turned squarely around to face him. "It's you! What part have you got in this?"

Ross shrugged. "None at all. Just wonderin'. Everywhere I been, if a man is attacked an' kills two men against his one, he's figured to be quite a man, not a lynchin' job."

"He killed a Box N man!"

"Sure." Ross smiled. "Box N men can die as well as any others. It was a fair shake from all I hear. All three had guns, all three did some shootin'. I haven't heard any Reynolds men kickin' because it was two against one. Kind of curious, that. I'm wonderin' why all the RR men are suddenly out of town?"

"You wonder too much!" It was the man from the springs. "This is none of your deal! Keep out of it!"

Ross Haney still leaned against the door, but his eyes turned to the man from the springs. Slowly, carefully, contemptuously he looked the rider over from head to heel, then back again. Then he said softly: "Pogue, you've got a taste for knick-knacks. If you want to take this boy home with you, keep him out of trouble."

The rider took a quick step forward. "You're not running any bluff on me, Haney!"

"Forget it, Voyle! You get to huntin' for Burt. I'll talk to Haney." Pogue's voice was curt.

Voyle hesitated, his right hand hovering over his gun, but Ross did not move, lounging carelessly against the doorpost, a queer half smile on his face.

With an abrupt movement then, Voyle turned away, speaking quickly over his shoulder. "We'll talk about it later, Haney!"

"Sure," Ross Haney said, and then as a parting he called softly: "Want to bring Dahl with you?"

Voyle caught himself in mid-stride, and Voyle's shoulders hunched as if against a blow. He stopped and stared back, shock, confusion, and puzzlement struggling for expression.

Haney looked back at Pogue. "You carry some characters," he said. "That Voyle now. He's touchy, ain't he?"

"What did you mean about Dahl? He's not one of my riders!"

"Is that right? I thought maybe he was, although I'll admit I didn't know."

Walt Pogue stared at him, annoyed and angry, yet puzzled, too. The big man walked back to the restaurant stove, got a cup, and poured coffee into it from the big coffee pot. He put sugar in it, and then cream. He glanced over his shoulder at Ross.

Haney felt a slight touch on his shoulder and glanced around and found May at his shoulder.

"He's gone!" she whispered. "He's not there."

There was dust on her dress and he slapped at it, and she hurriedly brushed it away. "Where was he shot?" he asked, under his breath.

"In the leg. He couldn't go far, I know."

Pogue turned around. "What are you two talking about?" he demanded. "Why the whispering?"

"Is it any of your business?" Haney said sharply.

Walt Pogue stiffened and put his cup down hard. "You'll go too far, Haney! Don't try getting rough with me! I won't take it!"

"I'm not askin' you to," Ross replied roughly. He straightened away from the door post. "I don't care how you take it. You're not running me or any part of me, and you might as well learn that right now. If I choose to whisper to a girl, I'm doin' it on my own time, so keep out of it."

Pogue stared at him, and then at the girl, and there was meanness in his eyes. He shrugged. "It's a small matter. With all this trouble I'm gettin' jumpy."

Voyle came back into the room accompanied by two other men. "No sign of him, boss. We've been all over the hotel. Simmons an' Clatt went through the vegetable cellar, too, but there ain't a sign of him. There was an empty box under those spuds, though, big enough to hide a man."

Allan Kinney had come back into the room.

"What about that, Kinney?" Pogue demanded.

"Probably somethin' to keep the spuds off the damp ground, much as possible," Haney suggested carelessly. "Seems simple enough."

Pogue's jaw set and he turned swiftly. "You, Haney! Keep out of this! I was askin' Kinney, not you!"

This time Voyle had nothing to say. Ross glanced at him, and the man looked hastily away. *He's scared,* Ross told himself mentally. *He's mixed in some deal and doesn't want his boys to know it. He's afraid I'll say too much.*

Pogue turned and strode from the restaurant, going out through the hotel lobby, his men trooping after him. When the last man was gone, May turned to Kinney. "Allan, where can he be? He was there, you know he was there!"

Kinney nodded. "I know." He twisted his hands together. "He must have heard them and got out somehow. But where could he go?"

Ross Haney was already far ahead of them. He was thinking rapidly. The searchers would probably stop for a drink, but they would not stop long. Voyle was apparently in on the plot to have Burt killed, for he had been at the springs, and this had happened too swiftly. Too little noise had come from the RR for it to be anything but a plot among them. Or so it seemed to Haney. For some reason Rolly Burt had become dangerous to them, and he was supposed to die in the gunfight the previous night, but had survived and killed one of their men and wounded another. Now he must be killed, and soon.

Yet Haney was thinking further than that. His

mind was going outside into the darkness, thinking of where he would go if he were a wounded man with little ammunition and no time to get away. He would have to hobble or to drag himself. He would be quickly noticed by anyone and quickly investigated. He would not dare go too far without shelter, for there was some light outside even though it was night.

Then Haney was recalling the stone wall. It started not far from the hotel stables and went around an orchard planted long ago. Some of the stones had fallen, but much of it was intact. A man might make a fair defense from behind that wall, and he could drag himself all of a hundred yards behind it.

Ross walked swiftly out of the hotel through the back door. There in the darkness he stood stockstill at the side of the door, letting his eyes become accustomed to the night. After a minute or two he could pick out the stable, the orchard, and the white of the stones in the wall.

Walking to the stable, he took the path along the side, then put a hand on the stone wall, and dropped over it with a quick vault. Then he stood still once more. If he approached Burt too suddenly, the wounded man might mistake him for an enemy and shoot. Nor did he know Burt, or Burt him.

Moving silently, Haney worked his way along the stone wall. It was no more than three feet high and along much of it there was a hedge of weeds and brambles. He ripped a scratch on his hand, then swore. Softly he moved ahead, and he was almost to the corner when a voice spoke, very low.

"All right, mister, you've made a good guess but a bad one. Let one peep out of you an' you can die."

"Burt?"

"Naw!" the cowhand was disgusted. "This is King Solomon an' I'm huntin' the Queen of Sheba! Who did you think it would be?"

"Listen, an' get this straight the first time. I'm your friend, and a friend of May's and Kinney's from the hotel. I've been huntin' you to help you out of here. There's a horse at May's shack, an' we've got to get you there just as fast as we can make it. You hear?"

"How do I know who you are?"

"I'd have yelled, wouldn't I? If I found you?"

"Oncet, maybe. No more than oncet, though. This Colt still carries a kick. Who are you? I can't see your face."

"I'm Ross Haney. Just blew in."

"The *hombre* that backed down Syd Berdue? Sure thing. I know you. Heard all about it. It was a good job."

"Can you walk?"

"I can take a stab at it if you give me a shoulder."

"Let's go then."

With an arm around Burt's waist, Haney got

him over the fence and then down the dark alleyway between it and the stone house next to it. They came out in an open space, and beyond it there was the trail, and then the woods. Once in the shelter of the trees they would have ample concealment all the way to May's house.

Yet once they were started across that open space, any door opened along the backs of the buildings facing them from across the street would reveal them and they would be caught in the open. There would be nothing for it then but to shoot it out.

"All right, Burt. Here we go! If any door opens, freeze where you are!"

"Where you takin' me?" Supporting himself with a hand on Haney's shoulder, and Haney's arm around his waist, he made a fair shift at hobbling along.

"May's shack. If anything delays me, get there. Take her horse an' light out. You know that old trail to the badlands?"

"Sure, but it ain't no good unless you circle around to Thousand Springs. No water. An' that's one mighty rough ride."

"Don't worry. I'll handle that. You get over there and find a spot to watch the trail until you see me. But with luck we'll make it together."

Burt's grip on Haney's shoulder tightened. "Watch it! Somebody openin' that door."

They stopped, standing stockstill. Ross felt

Burt's off arm moving carefully, and then he saw the cowhand had drawn a gun. He was holding it across his stomach, covering the man who stood in the light of the open door. It was a saloon bartender.

Somebody loomed over the fat bartender's shoulder. "Hey! Who's that out there?"

"Go on back to your drinks," the bartender said. "I'll go see." He came down the steps and stalked out toward them, and Haney slid his hand down for his left gun.

The fat man walked steadily toward them until he was close by. He glanced from one face to the other. "Pat," Burt said softly, "you'd make a soft bunk for this lead."

"Don't fret yourself," he said. "If I hadn't come, one of those drunken Box N riders would have, an' then what? You shoot me, an' you have them all out here. Go on, beat it. I'm not huntin' trouble with any side." He looked at Haney. "Nor with you, Ross. You don't remember me, but I remember you right well from your fuss with King Fisher. Get goin' now."

He turned and strode back to the door.

"What is it?" A drunken voice called. "If it's Rolly Burt, I'll fix him!"

"It ain't. Just a Mex kid with a horse. Some stray he picked up, an old crow-bait. Forget it!"

The door closed.

Ross heaved a sigh. Without further talk, they

110

moved on, hobbling across the open, then into the trees. There they rested. They heard a door slam open. Men came out into the street and started up the path away from them. They had been drinking and were angry. The town of Soledad would be an unpleasant place on this night.

When Haney had the mare saddled, he helped Rolly up. "Start down the trail," he said. "If you hear anybody comin', get out of sight. When I come, I'll be ridin' that Appaloosa of mine. You've seen it?"

"Sure. I'll know it. I keep goin' until you catch up, right?"

"Right. Keep out of sight of anybody else, and I mean *anybody*. That goes for your RR hands as well. Hear me?"

"Yeah, an' I guess you're right at that. They sure haven't been much help. But I'll not forget what you've done, a stranger, too."

"You ride. Forget about me. I've got to get back into Soledad an' get my horse out without excitin' comment. Once I get you where I'm takin' you, nobody will find you."

He watched the mare start up the road at a fast walk, and then he turned back toward the town.

He heard shouts and yells, and then a drunken cowhand blasted three shots into the air.

Ross Haney hitched his guns into place and started down the road into Soledad. He was walking fast.

IX

The disappearance of Rolly Burt was a nine-day wonder in the town of Soledad and the Ruby Hills. Ross Haney, riding in and out of town, heard the question discussed and argued from every standpoint. Burt had not been seen in Rico, nor in Pie Town. Nor had any evidence of him been found on the trails. No horses were accounted missing, and the search of the Box N cowhands had been fruitless. Neither Allan Kinney nor May asked any questions of Ross, although several times he recognized their curiosity.

The shooting and the frenzied search that followed had left the town abnormally quiet. Yet the rumor was going around that with the end of the coming roundup, the whole trouble would break open again and be settled, once and for all. For the time being, with the roundup in the offing, both ranches seemed disposed to ignore the feud and settle first things first.

Second only to the disappearance of Rolly Burt was Ross Haney himself as a topic of conversation. He spent money occasionally, and he came and went around Soledad, but no one seemed to have any idea what he was doing, or what his plans were. Curiosity was growing, and the three most curious men were Walt Pogue, Chalk

Reynolds, and Star Levitt. There was another man even more curious, and that one was Emmett Chubb.

It was after the disappearance of Burt that Chubb first heard of Haney's presence in the Ruby Hills. The RR hands ate at one long table presided over by Chalk himself, and Syd Berdue sat always at his right hand.

"Heard Walt Pogue an' his man Voyle had some words with that Haney," Reynolds said to Berdue. "Looks like he's gettin' this country buffaloed."

Berdue went white to the lips and started to make an angry reply when he was cut off by the sudden movement down the table. Emmett Chubb had lunged to his feet. The stocky, hardfaced gunman leaned across the table. "Did you say Haney?" he rasped. "Would that be Ross Haney?"

"That's right." Reynolds looked up sharply. "Know him?"

Chubb sat back in his chair with a thud. "I should smile I know him. He's a-huntin' me."

"You?" Reynolds stared. "Why?"

Chubb shrugged. "Me an' a friend of his had a run-in. You knew him. Vin Carter."

"Ah? Carter was a friend of Haney's?" Reynolds chewed in silence. "How good is this Haney?"

"He thinks he's plumb salty. I wouldn't be for

knowin', however. Down thataway they sure set store by him."

A slim, dark-faced cowhand looked up and drawled softly: "I know him, Emmett, an', when you tangle with him, be ready. He's the *hombre* who went into King Fisher's hide-out in Mexico after a horse one of Fisher's boys stole off him. He rode the horse out, too, an' the story is that he made Fisher take water. He killed the *hombre* who stole his horse. The fellow was a fool half-breed who went for his gun."

"So he's chasin' you, Emmett?" Reynolds muttered. "Maybe that accounts for his bein' here."

"An' maybe he's here because of Vin Carter," Berdue said. "If he is, that spells trouble for Pogue. That won't hurt us any."

In the days that had followed the escape of Rolly Burt, Haney had not been idle. He had thrown and branded several of the wild cattle, and had pushed a few of them out into the open valley below Thousand Springs. There would be plenty of time later to bring more of them; all he wanted was for the brand to show up when the roundup was under way.

Astride the Appaloosa, he headed for the VV. The morning was warm, but pleasant, and he rode down into the shade under the giant old cotton-woods feeling very fit and very happy. Several of the hands were in sight, and one of them was the slope-shouldered Dahl, mending a saddle girth.

Bob Vernon saw him and his brow puckered in a slight frown. He turned and walked toward Ross Haney. "Get down, won't you? Sherry has been telling me something about you."

"Thanks, I will. Is she here?" His purpose had been to verify, if he could, some of his ideas about that conversation he had seen and she had overheard at the springs. Also, he was curious about the set-up at the VV. It was the one place he had not catalogued in his long rides.

"Yes," Vernon hesitated, "she's here." He made no move to get her. Suddenly he seemed to make a decision. "I say, Haney. You're not coming with the idea of courting my sister, are you? You know she's spoken for."

"That idea," Haney said grimly, "seems to be one everyone wants to sell me. First heard it from Star Levitt."

Vernon's lips tightened. "You mean Star talked to you about Sherry?"

"He did. And Sherry told me she was to marry him."

Bob Vernon appeared relieved. He relaxed. "Well, then you understand how things are. I wouldn't want any trouble over her. Star's pretty touchy."

"Understand this." Haney turned sharply around and faced Bob. "I was told that by Levitt and by Sherry. Frankly the fact that she is engaged to him doesn't make a lot of difference to me. I haven't told that to her, but you're her brother, and I'm tellin' you. You don't need any long-winded explanations about how I feel about her. When I'm sure she's in love with him, I'll keep away. Until then, I'm in to stay."

Surprisingly Vernon did not get angry. He appeared more frightened and worried. "I was afraid of that," he muttered. "I should have known."

"Now, if you won't get her for me, I'll go to the house after her."

"After whom?" They turned swiftly to see Sherry walking toward them, smiling. "Hello, Ross. Who were you coming after? Who could ever make your voice sound like that?"

"You," he said bluntly. "Nobody but you."

Her smile vanished, but there was warmth in her eyes. "That's nice," she said. "You say it as if you mean it."

"I do."

"Boss?" A tall, lean, and red-headed cowhand had walked up to them, and, when they turned, he asked: "Who has the Gallows Frame brand?"

"Gallows Frame?" Vernon shrugged. "Never heard of it. Where did you see it?"

"Up toward Thousand Springs. Seen several mighty fine-lookin' bulls an' a few cows up that-away an' all wearin' that brand, a gallows frame with a ready noose hangin' from it. An' them cows, why they are wilder'n all get out. Couldn't get anywhere near 'em."

"That's something new," Vernon commented. "Have you seen any of them, Sherry?"

She shook her head, but there was a strange expression in her eyes. She glanced over at Ross Haney, who listened with an innocence combined with humor that would have been a perfect giveaway to anyone who knew him.

"No, I haven't seen any of them, Bob." She looked at the redhead again. "Mabry, have you met Ross Haney? He's new around here, but I imagine he's interested in brands."

Mabry turned to Haney and grinned. "Heard somethin' about you," he said. "Seems you had a run-in with Syd Berdue."

Ross noted that Kerb Dahl's fingers had almost ceased to move in their work on the girth.

Mabry walked away with Bob Vernon, and Sherry turned to Ross, her eyes cool but friendly. "I thought you might be interested in knowing Bill Mabry. He was always a good friend of that cowhand they were looking for in town . . . Rolly Burt."

Haney's eyes shifted to her thoughtfully. There seemed to be very little this girl did not know. She would be good to have for a friend, and not at all good as an enemy. She was as intelligent as she was beautiful. Her eyes never seemed asleep, for she seemed to see everything and to comprehend what she was seeing. Was that a lucky guess about Burt? Or did she know? Would Kinney have told her?

Of course, he recalled, Kinney had said she had suggested him. That might be it. She was guessing.

Dahl's ears were obviously tuned to catch every word, so he turned. "Shall we walk over and sit down?" He took her elbow and guided her to a seat under one of the huge cottonwoods.

"Sherry," he said suddenly, "I told Bob I didn't intend to pay no attention to this engagement of yours unless I found out you were in love with Levitt. Are you?"

She looked away quickly, her face suddenly pale and her lips tight. Finally she spoke. "Why else would a girl be engaged to a man?"

"I haven't any idea. There might be reasons." He stared at her, and then his eyes strayed to Dahl. "Until you tell me you do, and look me in the eye when you say it, I'm goin' ahead. I want you, Sherry. I want you like I never wanted anything in this world, an' I mean to have you if you could care for me. I'm not askin' you now. Just tellin' you. When I came into this valley, I came expectin' trouble, an' I thought I knew all the angles. Well, I've found out there's somethin' more goin' on here than I expected, an' it's somethin' you know about.

"Maybe you don't know it all. I'm bankin' you don't. You heard me talkin' to myself. Well, what I said then goes. I'm here alone, an' I'm ridin' for my own brand, an' you've guessed right, for that

Gallows Frame is mine, an' the noose is for any-body who wants to hang on it. The RR spread an' the Box N are controlled by a couple of range pirates. They whipped and murdered smaller, weaker men to get what they've got. If they keep it, they'll know they've been in a fight."

Sherry had listened intently. Her face had become serious. "You can't do anything alone, Ross. You must have help." She put her hand on his arm. "Ross, is Rolly safe? Understand, I am not asking you where he is, just if he is safe. He did me a good turn once, and he's an honest man."

"He's safe. For your own information, and not to be repeated, he's workin' for me now. But he can't do much for another ten days or more, an' by that time it may be too late. Can I rely on Mabry?"

"You can. If he will work for you, he will die for you, and kill for you if it's in the right kind of fight. He was Burt's best friend."

"Then, if I can talk to him, you'll lose a hand." He looked down at her. "Sherry, what's goin' on here? Who is Star Levitt? Who are those men I saw in town? This Kerb Dahl here, and Voyle? I know there's some connection."

She got up quickly. "I can't talk about that. Star Levitt is going to be my husband."

Ross got up, too. Roughly he picked up his hat and jerked it on his head, then stood there, hands on hips, staring at her.

119

"Not Levitt!" he said harshly. "Well, if you won't tell me, I'll find out, anyway."

He turned abruptly, and saw the two men he had seen in town at the restaurant—Kerb Dahl and the shorter, hard-faced man.

In that single instant he became aware of many things. Bob Vernon stood in the door, white as death. Kerb Dahl, a hard gleam in his eyes, was on the right and he walked with elbows bent, hands swinging at his gun butts. Behind them Haney could see the big, old tree with a bench around it, and a rusty horseshoe nailed to the trunk. Two saddled horses stood near the corral, and the sunlight through the leaves dappled the earth with shadow.

Behind him there was a low moan of fear from Sherry, but he did not move, only waited and watched the two men coming toward him. It could be here. It could be now. It could be at this moment.

Dahl spoke first, his lean, cadaverous face hard and with a curiously set expression. The shorter man had moved apart from him a little. Haney remembered the girl behind him, and knew he dare not fight—but some sixth sense warned him that somewhere else would be a third man, probably with a rifle. The difference.

Kerb Dahl spoke. "You're Ross Haney. I reckon you know me. I'm Dahl, an' this here is the first time you've come to the VV, an' this is goin' to be the last. You come on this place again an' you get killed. We don't aim to have no troublemakers around."

Ross Haney held very still, weighing his next words carefully. This could break into a shooting match in one instant. "Then have your artillery ready when I come back," he warned them. "Because, when I'm ready, I'll come back."

"We told you."

Ross looked them over coldly, knowing they had expected to find him as tough and ready for a fight as he had been with Chalk Reynolds and Berdue. Yet there was a queer sense of relief in their eyes, too. Haney guessed that, while there must be a hidden rifleman, these men were afraid for their skins.

Mabry stood nearby as Ross swung into the saddle. "I've got a job for you if you can get to town within the next twelve hours. At the saloon. You might run into a friend of yours."

Mabry did not reply, so Haney rode away, leaving the cowhand standing there. He had spoken softly enough so he knew he was not overheard. Yet Haney knew he was no closer to a solution than before.

There was danger here. An odd situation existed in the Ruby Hills. Scowling, he considered it. On the one hand was Walt Pogue with Bob Streeter and Repp Hanson, two notorious killers. On the other was Chalk Reynolds with Syd Berdue and Emmett Chubb.

Here at the VV was a stranger situation. Bob and Sherry Vernon, who owned the ranch, seemed completely dominated by Levitt and their own hands. Also Levitt had a strong claim of some kind on Sherry herself. What could be behind that? Scowling, Ross considered it. Whatever it was, it could mean everything to him, not only for his plans in the valley, but because of his love for Sherry.

Somewhere in this patchwork of conflicting interests, there was another grouping, that small band that had gathered at the springs with Syd Berdue. The band was made up of at least one man from each ranch—of Kerb Dahl of the VV, Voyle of the Box N, and Tolman of the Three Diamonds.

Where did this last group stand? Voyle, from his actions, wanted Pogue to know nothing of his tie-up with Dahl. Did Reynolds know about Burdue's meeting at the springs? Who was behind it?

X

Quiet reigned at the Bit and Bridle when Ross Haney rode into town in the late afternoon. He left his horse at the rail and strolled through the half doors to the cool interior.

Only Pat, the bartender, was present. The room was dusky and still. Pat idly polished glasses as he came in, glanced up at him, and then put a bottle and a glass on the bar. Ross leaned an elbow on the hardwood and dug out the makings. He built a smoke without speaking, liking the restfulness and coolness after his hot ride, and thinking over what he had seen at the VV.

"You've lived here a long time, Pat?"

"Uhn-huh. Before Carter was killed."

"Lots of changes?"

"Lots."

"There's goin' to be more, Pat."

"Room for 'em."

"Where do you stand?"

Pat turned sharply and fixed his eyes on Haney. "Not in the middle. Not with Reynolds or Pogue. As for you, I'm neither for you nor against you."

"That's plain enough." Haney didn't know whether to be pleased or angry. After Pat's attitude in regard to Burt, he had hoped he might be an ally. "But you don't sound like much help."

"That's right. No help at all. I've got my saloon. I'm doin' all right. I was here before Reynolds and Pogue. I'll be here after they are gone."

"And after I'm gone?"

"Maybe that, too." Pat suddenly turned again and rested his big hands on the bar. "You fool around with Pogue all you want. With Reynolds, too. But you lay off Levitt an' his crowd, you hear? They ain't human. They'll kill you. They'll eat you like a cat does a mouse, when they get ready."

"Maybe." Ross struck a match with his left hand. "Who are his crowd?"

Pat looked disgusted. "You've been to the VV. He runs that spread. Don't you be too friendly with that girl, either. She's poison."

Haney let that one ride. Maybe she was poison. Maybe feeling the way he did about her was the thing that would break him. He was a strong man. He had not lived that long under the conditions he knew without knowing his own strength and knowing how it compared with the strength of others. He knew that, when he was sure, he would push his luck to any degree, but as yet he was not pushing it, as yet no one in the valley knew his real intentions.

Pogue believed he had come looking for Chubb. Reynolds and Berdue, despite their hatred for him, believed he was after Pogue. Each was prepared to keep hands off in hopes he would injure the other. Yet the roundup was going to blow the lid off, for the roundup was going to show that he had cattle on the range, and had pitched his hat into the ring. Then he would be in the middle of the fight with every man's hand against him.

Pat's warning was right. Pogue and Reynolds

124

were dangerous, but nothing compared to Levitt's crowd. Lifting his glass, Ross studied his reflection in the mirror, the reflection of a tall, wide-shouldered young man with blunt, bronzed features and a smile that came easily to eyes that were half-cynical, half-amused. He was a tall young man with a flat-brimmed, flat-crowned black hat and a gray, shield-chested shirt and a black knotted kerchief, black crossed belts supporting the worn holsters and walnut-stocked guns. He was a fool, he decided, to think as he did about Sherry. What could he offer such a girl? On the other hand, what could Star Levitt offer her?

Regardless, he was here to stay. When he had raced the Appaloosa into the street of Soledad, he had come to remain. If he had to back it with gunfire, he would do just that. Carefully he considered the state of his plans. There was no fault to find there. In fact, he had progressed beyond where he had expected in that he had a friend, an ally, a man who would stay with him to the last ditch. He had Rolly Burt.

Camping on the mesa, the wounded man was rapidly knitting. They had talked much, and Burt had told him what to expect of the roundup. He knew the characters and personalities of the people of the Ruby Hills, and he knew something more of Pogue and Reynolds. Over nights beside the campfire they had yarned and argued and talked. Both of them had ridden for Charles Goodnight, both for John Chisum. They knew the same saloons in Tascosa and El Paso. Both had been over the trail to Dodge and to Cheyenne. Both had been in Uvalde and Laredo, and they talked the nights away of cattle and horses, of rustling and gunfighters until they knew each other, and knew they spoke the same language. Rolly had talked much of Mabry. He was a good man. While Mabry liked both Bob and Sherry Vernon, he had confided to Burt that he must leave the VV or be killed.

"Why were the Box N boys gunnin' for you, Rolly?" he had asked.

A frown had gathered between Rolly Burt's eyes. He had looked up at Ross over the fire. His blue eyes were puzzled and disturbed. "You know, I can't figure that. It was a set deal. I saw that right away. They'd been sent to murder me."

"How'd you happen to be in town?"

"Berdue sent me in for a message."

"I see." Ross had told him then about the meeting below the mesa, and everything but Sherry's part in it. "There's a tie-up there some-where. I think Berdue sent you on purpose, an' he had those Box N boys primed to kill you."

"But why?"

"Something you know, probably. The way I have it figured is that Syd Berdue is in some kind of a double-cross that he doesn't want Chalk to know about. Maybe he figured he'd tipped his hand somehow, and you knew too much. Voyle is in the deal with him, and I figured from the way he acted the other night in front of Pogue that he's double-crossing Walt. And I think Star Levitt is the man behind the whole thing."

"You mean a deal between Berdue and Levitt? But they are supposed to be on the outs."

"Sure, and what better cover-up? You keep an eye on the springs. They may meet again."

"Say!" Burt had glanced up. "Something I've been meaning to ask you. Several times I've heard a funny kind of rumbling, sounds like it comes out of the rock under me. You heard it?"

"Uhn-huh. Don't reckon it amounts to much, but someday we'll do some prowling. Kind of gives an *hombre* the shivers."

Standing now at the Bit and Bridle bar, Ross Haney went over that conversation. Yes, he was ahead of his plans in having such an ally as Rolly Burt.

He leaned his forearms on the hardwood and turned his head to glance out into the street. The rose of the setting sun had tinted the dusty, unpainted boards of the old building opposite with a dull glow, and beyond it, in the space between the buildings, a deep shadow had already gathered. At the rail, Río stamped his feet against a vagrant fly and blew contentedly.

It was a quiet evening. Suddenly he felt a

vague nostalgia, a longing for a home he had never known, the deep, inner desire for peace, his children about him, the quiet evening rest on a wide porch after a hard day on the range, and the sound of a voice inside, a voice singing. Yet, when he straightened and filled his glass again, the guns felt heavy against his legs. Someday, with luck, things would be different.

Then the half doors pushed open, and Star Levitt stood there, tall and handsome against the facing light. He looked for an instant at Ross, and then came on into the room. He wore the same splendid white hat, a white buckskin vest, and perfectly creased gray trousers tucked into polished boots. As always, the worn guns struck the only incongruous note. His voice was easy, confident.

"Buy you a drink?"

"Thanks, I've got one." In the mirror Ross's eyes caught the difference between them, his battered shabbiness against the cool magnificence of Levitt.

Levitt's smile was pleasant, his voice ordinary and casual. "Planning to leave soon?"

"No." Haney's voice was flat. "I'm never going to leave."

"That's what the country needs, they tell me. Permanent settlers, somebody to build on. It's a nice thought, if you can stick it."

"That's right. How about you, Levitt? Do you

think you'll be able to stick it when Reynolds and Pogue get to checking brands?" He heard a glass rattle in Pat's suddenly nervous fingers. He knew he had taken the play away from Levitt with that remark, and he followed it up. "I've been over the range lately, and there's a lot of steers out there with VVs made over into Three Diamonds, an' Box Ns to Triple Box As, an' I understand that brand happens to be yours, too."

Levitt had straightened and was looking at him, all the smile gone from his face. "You understand too much, Haney. You're getting into water that's too deep for you, or for any drifting cowhand."

"Am I? Let me judge. I've waded through some bad water a few times, an', where I couldn't wade, I could swim."

Star Levitt's eyes had widened and the bones seemed to stretch the skin of his face taut and hard. He was not a man used to being talked back to, and he wasn't used to being thwarted. He was shrewd, a planner, but in that instant Ross learned something else of him. He had a temper, and, when pushed, he got angry. Such a man was apt to be hasty. *All right,* Ross told himself, *let's see.*

"Another thing. You spoke the other day about a staked claim. I'm curious to see how deep your stakes are driven, so I'm going to find out for myself, Levitt. I don't think that claim is very secure. I think a little bit of bad weather an' all your stakes would shake loose. You're a big boy, Levitt, but you're not cutting the wide swath you think you are. Now you know where I stand, so don't try running any bluff on me. I won't take a pushing around."

"Stand aside, Star, an' let me have him!" The voice rang in an almost empty room, and Haney's hair prickled along his scalp as he saw Emmett Chubb standing just inside the door. "I want him, anyway, Star!"

Ross Haney stood, his feet wide apart, facing them and he knew he was in the tightest spot of his life. Two of the deadliest gunmen in the country were facing him, and he was alone. Cold and still he waited, and the air was so tense he could hear the hoarse breathing of the bartender beside him and across the bar.

So still was the air in the room that Bill Mabry's voice, low as it was, could be heard by all.

"If they want it, Haney, I'll take Star for you. He's right here under my gun."

Levitt's eyes did not waver. Haney saw the quick calculation in the big man's eyes, then saw decision. Levitt was sharp, and this situation offered nothing for anybody. It was two and two, and Mabry's position at the window from which he spoke commanded the situation perfectly, as he was just slightly behind both Levitt and Chubb.

It was Pat who broke the stalemate. "Nobody does any shootin' here unless it's me," he said flatly. "Mabry, you stand where you are. Chubb, you take your hand away from that gun an' get out of that door, face first. Star, you foller him. I ain't aimin' to put clean sawdust on this here floor again today. Now git!"

He enforced his command with the twin barrels of a shotgun over the edge of the bar, and nobody had any argument with a shotgun at close quarters. A six-gun warrants a gamble, but there is no gamble with a sawed-off scatter-gun.

Chubb turned on his heel and strode from the room, and Star smiled suddenly, but his eyes were cold as they turned to Haney. "You talk a good fight," he said. "We'll have to see what you're holding."

"All right," Ross replied shortly. "I'll help you check brands at the roundup!"

Levitt walked out, and then Bill Mabry put a foot through the open window, and stepped into the bar. He grinned. "That job open?"

Haney laughed. "Friend, you've been working for me for the last three minutes," he declared warmly.

"You two finish your drinks and pull out," Pat said dryly. "Powder smoke gives me a headache."

XI

Gathered over the fire in the hollow atop the mesa, crouched three men, not daring to use the partly constructed house as the glow of the fire might attract attention. Here, in a more sheltered position far back from the rim, they could talk in quiet and without fear of the fire attracting undue attention.

Burt, whose leg was much better, was cooking. "It ain't all clear, Ross, but I think you've got the right idea. It looks like Levitt is engineerin' some kind of a steal if Voyle, Dahl, an' Berdue are in it with him. I do know this. There's been a passel of hardcases comin' into the valley here lately. They ain't tied in with the Box N or the RR by any means."

"Sure, look at Streeter an' Hanson," Mabry said. "They are with Pogue, but how far can he count on 'em? I think Streeter an' Hanson will stay out of things if Levitt says to. I think he's cut the ground from under the feet of both men."

"Those brands I've looked at aren't intended to fool anybody, it seems to me," Haney commented. "I think Levitt plans to start trouble. It's my opinion that he'll blow the lid off things just when the rest of them are standin' by for the roundup. How many reliable hands has Vernon got?"

"Three or four," Mabry replied. "Dahl and his partner ran several off. A man sure don't feel comfortable workin' around a ranch with two *hombres* on the prod like that."

"What goes on around there?" Haney asked Mabry. "You've lived on that spread, an' should know."

Mabry shrugged. "I sure don't know," he said honestly. "Seems to be a lot of movin' around at night on that spread, but Dahl or his partner are usually by the door, an' they go out to see what it's all about. Several times at night riders have showed up there, leavin' hard-ridden horses behind when they take off. No familiar brands but one. That I think I've seen down Mexico way."

Ross took the plate he was handed and dished up some fríjoles and then accepted the coffee Burt poured for him. There seemed to be but one answer. He would have to do some night riding and look around a little. After all, there couldn't be many possibilities.

"Well," Burt suggested at last, "the roundup starts tomorrow. Before it has gone very far, we'll know a lot of things."

From the rim of the mesa they watched all the following morning. Reynolds's hands were rounding up cattle, driving them out of the timber and down into the flat. Some of the Box N riders were part of the group.

The weather was hot and dry, and dust arose in clouds. The cattle moved from the shade and ample water of the springs with reluctance. As always, it gave Ross a thrill to watch the cattle gathered and to see a big herd moving. He kept back and out of sight but took turns with Mabry at watching the work.

Regardless of their sympathies, there were good cattlemen on both sides. The riders got the cattle out of the brakes and started them down-valley to the accompaniment of many yells, much shouting back and forth, and the usual good-natured persiflage and joking that is part of any roundup crew. As far as Ross's glass was able to see, the same thing was happening every-where. There would be several thousand head of stock to work in this roundup, and it would move on down the range for many miles before com-pleted.

Mabry slid up alongside of him at noon on the second day. "You want me to rep for you, or will you tackle it your own self?"

Haney thought a minute. "We'll both go down, but we'll go loaded for bear. I think hell is going to break loose down there before many days."

"If they start to fight, what do we do?" Mabry asked keenly.

"Pull out. We don't have a battle with any of them. Not yet, we don't, but almost any of them might take a shot at us. When they see what's happened, that I've got cattle on this range, they aren't going to be too happy about it."

"Have you seen Scott?"

"Only for a minute or two. He's advisin' me to get more hands, but I don't want anybody killed, neither of you nor myself, either. If there's only three of us, we'll play our cards the way we should, close to our belt. If there were more, we might take chances and get somebody killed. If they start a battle, pull out."

"Don't you rate that Levitt too low, Haney." Mabry shook his head seriously. "He's cold-blooded, and he'll do whatever he's a mind to, to get his way on this range. He hasn't any use for either Pogue or Reynolds, but he's a sight worse than either of them."

It was good advice, and the following day, when the two drifted down off the mesa toward the roundup, Ross Haney was thinking about it.

"Remember one thing," he advised Mabry. "We may not be together all the time. Don't let yourself get sucked in. Hold to the outer edge all the time, and keep an eye on the hands we've talked about who we believe to be tied in with Levitt. I wouldn't be surprised at anything. If they start scattering out, and seem to be taking up any definite positions, ease out of there quick."

Walt Pogue looked unhappy when he saw the two riding up. Then he brightened noticeably. "You two hunting work? I need some men."

135

"No." Haney noted that Chalk Reynolds was riding over. "I've come to rep for my brand."

Pogue's head came down and his eyes squinted. He leaned toward them, and his somewhat thick lips parted. "Did you say . . . *your* brand?"

"That's right . . . the Gallows Frame."

The big rancher's face went white, then darkened with a surge of blood. He reined his horse around violently. "Who said you could run cattle on this range?"

Ross Haney shrugged. Chalk Reynolds looked as astonished and angry as Pogue. "Does anybody have to say so? Strikes me this here is government land, and my stock has as much right to run on it as yours, an' maybe more right."

"You'll find there's a difference of opinion on that!" Chalk Reynolds put in violently. "This range is overcrowded now."

"Tell that to Star Levitt. He's on it with two brands."

This was obviously no news to either of them, but neither had anything to say for a minute, and then Reynolds said coldly: "Well, he'll be told! From what I hear, somebody's doin' some mighty smooth work with a cinch ring!"

Ross hooked his leg around the saddle horn and began to dig for the makings. "Reynolds, if you an' Pogue will take a look at those altered brands, you'll see that whoever altered them doesn't give a hoot whether you know it or not. He's throwin' it right in your face, an'askin' what you intend to do."

"I'll do plenty!" Chalk bellowed. "There's goin' to be a new set-up on this range after this roundup is over!"

"You throwin' that at me?" Pogue demanded. Fury was building in the man, and he was staring at Reynolds with an ugly light in his eye.

"Why don't you two either go to it or cut it out?" Haney drawled. "Or are you both afraid of Levitt? He's the *hombre* who's cuttin' in on you. He doesn't even bother to bring his own cows, he brands yours."

Ross chuckled, and Reynolds's face went white. He turned and said flatly, the rage trembling behind his even tones: "We might get together, Walt an' I, long enough to get shut of you!"

"Take first things first," Ross said. "An' you'd better learn this right now, Chalk. An' you, too, Pogue. I came here to stay. If you fellows stay here, it will be with me alongside of you. If you go, I'll still be here. I didn't come to this valley by chance. I came here on purpose, and with a definite idea in mind. Any bet you make, I'll double and raise. So any time you want to get into the game with me, just start the ball rolling, anyway you like."

He struck a match and lighted his smoke, then

dropped his leg back and kicked his foot into the stirrup. Coolly, and without a backward glance, he rode away.

Bill Mabry sat quietly for a minute or two, watching him ride.

Pogue glared at him. "What's in this, Bill? You've always been a good man."

"You listen to him," Mabry advised dryly. "He's *mucho malo hombre*, if you get what I mean. But only when he's crossed. He's got no reason to like either of you, but he's got other things on his mind now. But in case either of you wonder where I stand. Me an' my six-gun, we stand right alongside of Ross Haney. And that's where you'll find Rolly Burt, too!"

"Burt?" Pogue's face flamed. "Where is that murderin' son-of-a-bitch?"

Bill Mabry turned, his hand on the cantle of the saddle: "Listen, why don't you find out why two of your men were gunning for him, Pogue? I'll bet a paint pony you don't know. An' why don't you, Chalk Reynolds, find out why none of your boys was in town that night to side Burt? Why did your nephew send him into town for a message?"

Mabry turned and cantered his horse over to Ross. "I gave 'em some more," he said briefly, and explained.

Haney chuckled. "Their ears will be buzzing for a week if they live that long. Some nice stock here, Bill, at that."

"How many head have you got out here?"

"Not many. Couple of dozen head is all. Just something to make them unhappy."

"Suppose they start to get sore? Reynolds an' Pogue both can be mighty mean."

"We'll get meaner. I've got them cold-decked, Bill. Someday I'll tell you about it. I've got them all cold-decked. The only way they can beat me in the long run is with hot lead."

"Maybe. But that Star Levitt is poison."

"You think Pogue and Reynolds will get through the roundup without a fight?"

"No. There's too much hard feelin' amongst the boys. Somebody will blow his top and then the whole thing will bust up in a shootin' match."

Ross Haney looked across the valley, watching the familiar scene with a little of the old lift within him. This was the roundup, the hardest work in a cowhand's life, and in many ways the highest point. They cussed the roundup, and loved it. It was hot, dusty, full of danger from kicking hoofs and menacing horns, but filled with good fellowship and comradely fun.

The waving sea of horns tossed and rolled and fell as the cattle milled or the herd, starting to line out for somewhere, anywhere, was turned back on itself by some cowhand quick to stop the movement. At such times the horns would send a long ripple of movement across the herd.

Wild-eyed steers lunged for a getaway, but

were quickly harried back into the herd. At the branding pens men were gathered, the sharp line of demarcation between the RR and Box N a little broken here by the business of the day. Elsewhere, the men from the two big outfits drew off by themselves, worked together, and avoided contact with the rival ranch hands.

Star Levitt, astride a magnificent white horse, was everywhere to be seen. For a time, he was at the branding pens, and then he was circling the herd. Finally, sighting Ross Haney and Mabry, he walked his horse toward them. Ross saw Mabry stiffen and his face tighten and grow cold. Certainly there was no love lost here.

"How are you, Haney?" Levitt was easy, casual. He seemed to have forgotten completely the events of the day in the Bit and Bridle. He was clean-shaven as always, and as always he was immaculate. The dust of the roundup seemed scarcely to have touched him.

Mabry, glancing at the two, was struck for the first time at something strikingly similar in the two men, only there was a subtle difference that drew the cowhand inexorably to Ross Haney. Both were big men, Levitt the taller and heavier, and probably somewhat softer. Ross was lean and hard, his rugged build seeming so lean as to belie his actual weight, which was some 200 pounds. Yet in the faces of both men there was the look of command. Haney's manner was easy, even careless, yet there was something solid about him, something rock-like that was lacking in the brittle sharpness of Star Levitt.

These two were shaped by nature to be enemies, two strong men with their faces turned in the same direction, yet backed by wholly varied thinking. The one ruthless and relentless, willing to take any advantage, willing to stop at nothing. The other, hard, toughened by range wars and fighting, with the rough-handed fair play of the Western plains, yet equally relentless. It could be something, Mabry thought, if they ever came together in physical combat.

Ross began building a smoke. "Looks like a good herd. You got many cows here?"

"Quite a few." Levitt glanced at him sharply. "I hear you have some, too. That you're running the Gallows Frame brand."

"That's right." Ross lighted his smoke and eased his seat on the Appaloosa. "It's a good brand."

"Seems so. Strange that I hadn't heard of any cattle coming into the country lately. Did you pick yours up on the range?"

At many times in many places such a remark would have meant shooting. After Haney's equally insulting remarks in the Bit and Bridle, they were not important. These two knew their time was coming, and neither was in a rush. Levitt was completely, superbly confident. Ross was hard and determined, his hackles raised by this man, his manner always verging on outright aggressiveness.

"No, I didn't need to. Your pattern suits you, mine suits me." He inhaled deeply and let the smoke trickle out through his nostrils. "My cattle were already here."

The remark drew the response he wanted. It was a quick, nervous, and irritable scowl from Levitt. "That's impossible!" he said. "Only three brands ran on this range until I moved in!"

Haney smiled, knowing his enigmatic smile and manner would infuriate Levitt. "Star," he drawled, "you're an *hombre* that figures he's right smart, an' you might be if you didn't figure the other fellow was so all-fired dumb. A man like you ain't got a chance to win for long in any game for that reason. You take everybody for bein' loco or dumb as a month-old calf. You ride into everything full of confidence an' sneers. You're like most crooks. You think everything will turn out right for you. Why, you're so wrong it don't need any argument. You came into this country big an' strong. You were goin' to be the boss. You saw Reynolds an' Pogue, an' you figured them for easy marks. You maybe had something on the Vernons. I haven't figured that out yet, but like so many crooks you overlooked the obvious.

"Let me tell you something, my cut-throat

142

friend, an' get it straight. You lost this fight before you started. You might win with bullets, that's still anybody's guess, but you'll lose. You're smart in a lot of ways, an', if you were really smart you'd turn that horse of yours and start out of this country an' never stop until you're five hundred miles east of Tascosa."

Levitt smiled, but the smile was forced. For the first time the big man was uneasy, yet it was only for a moment. "I may not be as smart as I think, Haney, but no four-bit cowhand is going to out-smart me."

Ross turned slightly. "Bill, let's drift down toward the pens. I want to see what Reynolds an' Pogue think of those altered brands."

XII

Nonchalantly Haney turned his back on Levitt and started away. Mabry rode beside him, occasionally stealing a glance his way. "Boss, you're sure turnin' the knife in that *hombre*. What you aimin' to do, force his hand?"

"Somethin' like that. It does me good just to goad him. But you keep your eyes open, because he's got something cookin' now. I only wish"— his brow creased with worry—"I knew what he had on the Vernons. You don't suppose she really cares for that *hombre*, do you?"

Mabry shrugged. "I can guess what a fool cow

will do, an' I can outguess a bronc', but keep me away from women. I never could read the sign right to foller their trail. Just when you think you can read the brand, they turn the other way an' it looks altogether different."

Despite the growing sense of danger, the roundup was moving very well, yet the tenseness of the riders for all the brands was becoming increasingly evident. Several times Ross saw Sherry, but she avoided him. Bob Vernon was there, working like any of his men, and showing himself to be a fair hand, and a very willing one. Yet, as his eyes roved the herd and searched the faces of the riders, Ross could see that under the heat, the irritating, confusing dust, and the hard labor tempers were growing short.

On the third day, when the roundup had moved to the vicinity of Soledad, the break came. Ross had been trying to find a chance to talk to Sherry, and suddenly he saw it. The girl had been talking with Levitt. She had started away from him, riding toward the cottonwoods that marked the VV ranch house.

Ross started after her, and noticed Kerb Dahl, his hard, lupine face set grimly, staring after him. Dahl had drawn aside from the crowd and was building a smoke. Mabry, who had been working hard all morning, was still in the center of things, but Voyle was saddling a fresh horse.

Haney overtook Sherry and she looked up at

144

him. He noticed for the first time how thin she had grown and how white her face was.

"Sherry?" Surprisingly his voice was unsteady. "Wait a minute."

She drew up, waiting for him, but he thought she waited without any desire for conversation. She said nothing as he rode alongside. "Leaving so soon?"

She nodded. "Star said the men were getting pretty rough in their talk, and they'd be more comfortable if I went in."

"I've been hoping I'd have a chance to talk to you. You've been avoiding me." His eyes were accusing, but bantering.

She looked at him directly then. "Yes, Ross, I have. We must not see each other again. I'm going to marry Star, and seeing you won't do."

"You don't love him." The statement was flat and level, but she avoided his glance, and made no response. Then suddenly she said: "Ross, I've got to go. Star insisted I leave right away."

Haney's eyes hardened. "Do you take orders from him? What is this, anyway? Are you a slave? Haven't you a chance to make up your own mind?" Her face reddened and she was about to make a quick, and probably angry retort, when her remark hit him. He seized her wrist. "Sherry, you say Star insisted? That you leave *now?*"

"Yes." She was astonished and puzzled by his expression. "He said. . . ."

The remark trailed off, for Ross Haney had turned sharply in his saddle. Kerb Dahl had finished his cigarette. Voyle was fumbling with his saddle girth, and for the first time Haney noticed that he carried a rifle in his saddle scabbard, a rifle within inches of his hands. Ross's eyes strayed for the white horse, and found it on the far side.

He turned quickly. "Sherry, he's right. Get back to the ranch as fast as you can, and don't leave it!"

He wheeled his horse and started back toward the branding pens at a rapid canter, hoping he would be in time. A small herd of cattle was drifting down toward the pens, and behind it were Streeter and Repp Hanson.

As he drew up on the edge of the branding, Mabry was just straightening up from slapping a brand on a steer. "Bill!" Haney had to call three times before Mabry heard him, and then the red-headed cowhand turned and walked toward him. "Look out, Bill! It's coming."

His remark might have been a signal, for Emmett Chubb, sitting his horse near the corral on the outside of the pole fence, spoke up and pointed his remark at Riggs, a Box N rider. "You all feet, or just nat'rally dumb?"

Riggs looked up sharply. "What's the matter with you, Chubb? I haven't seen you down here doin' any work!"

Riggs was a slim, hard-faced youngster and a top hand. His anger was justifiable and he was not thinking or caring who or what Chubb was. Riggs had worked while the gunman lounged in his saddle, carrying his perpetual sneer.

"Shucks," Chubb said, "you Box N hands done enough work afore the roundup, slappin' brands on everythin' in sight! Bunch of tinhorn cow thieves!"

"You're a liar!" Riggs snapped, and Chubb's hand flashed for his gun. At that, Riggs almost made it. His gun was coming up when Chubb's first shot smashed him in the middle. He staggered back, gasping fiercely, struggling to get his gun up.

Instantly the branding pens were bursting with gunfire. Mabry swung into the saddle and whipped his horse around the corner of the stock pens, and he and Ross Haney headed for the timber. "It's their fight," Mabry said bitterly. "Let them have it."

"Look!" Haney was pointing.

Mabry glanced over his shoulder as the firing burst out, and his face went hard and cold.

Streeter and Hanson from their saddles had opened up on Reynolds and Pogue. Voyle was firing over the saddle of his horse, and cattle were scattering in every direction. Dust arose in a thick cloud. From it came the scream of a man in agony, then another burst of firing.

Mabry gasped out an oath. The freckles were standing out against the dead white of his face. "Pogue's own men turned on him!"

"Yeah." Ross Haney hurled his cigarette into the dust. "We'd better light a shuck. I think they intended to get us, too!"

The crash of guns stopped suddenly, but the scene was obscured by dust from the crazed cattle and excited horses. Ross saw a riderless horse, stirrups flapping, come from the dust cloud, head high and reins trailing. Behind them there was a single shot, then another.

Finally, with miles behind them, Mabry looked over at Ross. "I feel like a coyote ridin' away from a fight, like that, but it sure wasn't none of ours."

Haney nodded grimly. "I saw it comin' but never guessed it would break out just like that. It couldn't be stopped without killin' Levitt."

"You think he engineered it?"

"Sure." Haney explained how Levitt had started Sherry home, and how his riders had moved out of the workingmen's group to good firing positions. "Chubb had his orders. He deliberately started that fight when he got the signal."

"I'll get him if it's the last thing I do!" Mabry said bitterly. "That Riggs was a good hand. We hunted strays together."

"There was nothing we could have done but

stay there an' die. We've got other things to do, Bill. We've got to see that Levitt's plans go haywire an' that he gets his desserts. We've got to get the Vernons out from under. Star will have this country sewed up now, with no one able to buck him but us. He'll rave when he finds we got away."

"As far as Reynolds an' Pogue," Mabry said, "I can't feel no sorrow. They were a couple of murderin' wolves, but they had some good men ridin' for 'em." Mabry scowled. "Wonder what Levitt will do now? He's got the range sewed up with them two out of the way an' the Vernons knucklin' under to him."

Ross frowned. He had thought that over and believed he knew the answer. "That we'll have to wait an' see," he said. "I'm right curious myself. He'll hunt us, an' we'll have to lay low. He'll blame the whole thing on the feud between the two big outfits an' claim he was just an innocent bystander."

"What about the riders?" Mabry protested. "Some of them will tell the truth!"

"Bill," Haney said, "I'd lay a good bet none of them know. We knew pretty well what was comin', an' moreover we got off to one side with a clear view. Down there among the stampedin' cows, the dust, an' shootin', I'll bet the ones who are alive won't know. Moreover, I'll bet most of them drift out of the country. If they don't drift,

Levitt will probably see that they do. From his standpoint it's foolproof. Remember, too, that Levitt's gunmen were men from both outfits."

"If he kills like that," Mabry asked, "what chance have three men got?"

"The best chance, Bill. We're still honest men even if the only law is gun law. We'll wait an' see what Levitt does, but I imagine the first thing he'll do will be to clean up the loose ends. He may even call in the law from outside so he'll be in the clear with a clean bill of health."

Rolly Burt was waiting for them when they rode in. "What happened?" he demanded. "Did the lid blow off? I heard shootin'."

Briefly Haney explained. "The fight would have come, I expect, even if Levitt hadn't planned it."

"How many were killed?"

"No tellin'. I doubt if so many. Enough to warrant Levitt playin' the big, honest man who wants to keep the peace. Down there in the dust, I doubt if anybody scored many good shots. Too much confusion and too many running cattle. Riggs is probably dead."

"Murderin' coyotes!" Burt limped to the fire. "Set and eat. I've got the grub ready."

He dished up the food, then straightened, fork in hand. "Ross, what happened to Chalk?"

Haney did not look up. "He's sure to be dead. So's Pogue. Even Syd Berdue was shootin' at them. Killed his own uncle, or lent a hand."

"Chalk was no good, but no man deserves that." Burt looked up suddenly. "Boss, while you two were gone, I done some stumpin' around to loosen the muscles in this here game leg, an' guess what I found?"

"What?" Haney dished up a forkful of beans, then looked over it at Rolly, struck by something in his tone.

"That rumblin' in the rock . . . I found what causes it!" he said. "An' man, when you see it, your hair'll stand on end, I'm tellin' you!"

XIII

Yawning, Ross Haney opened his eyes to look through the aspen leaves at a cloudless sky. The vast expanse of blue stretched above them as yet unfired by the blazing heat of the summer sun. He rolled out of his soogan and dressed, trying to keep his feet out of the dew covering the grass.

Bill Mabry stuck a head bristling with red hair, all standing on end, out of his blankets and stared unhappily at Haney.

"Rolly," he complained, "what can a man do when his boss gets up early? It ain't neither fittin' nor right, I say."

"Pull your head back in then, you sorrel-topped bronc'!" Haney growled. "I'm goin' to have a look at the valley, an' then Rolly can roll out an' scare up some chuck."

"How about this all-fired rumblin'?" Mabry sat up. "I heard it again last night. Gives a man the creeps."

Burt sat up and looked around for his boots. He rubbed his unshaven jowls as he did every morning and muttered: "Dang it, I need a shave!"

"Never seen you when you didn't." Mabry thrust his thumb through a hole in his sock and swore, then pulled it on. "You need a haircut, too, you durned Siwash. Ugly, that's what you are! What a thing to see when you first wake up! Lucky you never hitched up with no girl. She sure would have had you curried and combed to a fare-thee-well!"

Ross left them arguing and, picking up his glass, walked to the nest of boulders he used for a lookout. Settling down on his stomach in the sand, he pointed the glass down the valley.

At first, all seemed serene and beautiful. The morning sunlight sparkled on the pool below, and the sound of the running water came to his ears. Somewhere, far off, a cow bawled. He swept the edge of the trees close at hand, studied the terrain below, and then bit by bit he eased his line of quest up until he was looking well down-range toward the Soledad trail.

The sun felt good on his back, and he squirmed to shift his position a little, leveled the glass, then froze.

A group of horsemen was coming up the trail

toward Thousand Springs, riding slowly. Star Levitt, he made out, was not among them. As they drew nearer, he picked out first one, and then another. They were led by Syd Berdue, and Kerb Dahl and Voyle were with him. Also, Emmett Chubb and half a dozen other riders. As they drew rein below him and let their horses drink, a few words drifted up to him.

This time they were making no secret of their conversation, and in the bright morning air their words were, for the most part, plain enough.

"Beats all where he got to!" Dahl replied. "I never did see Star so wrought up about anythin' as when he found they'd got away. He must have turned over everything in the flat, a-huntin' 'em. Refused to believe they'd got away. Golly was he mad!"

"He's a bad man to cross," Streeter commented. "I never seen him mad before. He goes crazy."

Chubb hung at one edge of the group, taking no part in their talking. His eyes strayed toward Berdue from time to time. Finally he swung down and walked to one of the springs for a drink, and, when he came back, wiping his mouth, his eyes shifted from one to the other. "Some things about this I don't like," he said.

There was no reply. Watching, Ross had the feeling that Chubb expressed the view of more than one of them. Syd idly flicked his quirt at a mesquite.

"Well, you can't say he ain't thorough," he said grimly.

Chubb looked around. "Yeah," he agreed sarcastically. "But how thorough? Where does his bein' thorough stop? You ever start to figure like that? He had me primed to start the play by gunnin' Riggs, as he had Riggs pegged as a hot head who would go for a gun if pushed. Well, I hadn't no use for Riggs my ownself, but he never told me what was to come after. It was pure luck I didn't get killed."

"Where did you reckon Haney went?" Dahl demanded, changing the subject.

"Where did Rolly Burt go?" Voyle asked. "You ask me, that Ross Haney is nobody's fool. He an' Mabry sure got shut of those brandin' pens in a hurry. They lit out like who flunk the chunk. Maybe left the country."

"He shore didn't," Chubb said bitterly. "He wants my scalp. He'll not leave if I read his tracks right."

"He called the boss a couple of times," Voyle said. "Pogue, too. Don't seem to take no water for anybody."

Syd Berdue's eyes shifted from face to face, waiting for somebody to mention his own fuss with Haney, but they avoided his eyes. "I'd say the thing to do would be to stop chasin' over the country an' keep an eye on that Kinney feller. He was right friendly with Haney, they tell me."

"Or Sherry Vernon," Dahl sneered. "I think the boss is buckin' a stacked deck with her."

Watching from the mesa, and listening to the faint sound of their voices, Ross could see Kerb Dahl's eyes shifting from man to man. He shook his own head, disgusted. *They talk too much,* he told himself. *That Dahl will tell Levitt every word or I miss my guess. He wasn't planted on the VV for nothing.*

Long after the group rode away, he lay there restlessly, hoping for some sight of Sherry, but there was none. More than he cared to admit, he was worried about her. Star Levitt had been revealed as a much more ruthless man, and a more cruel man than he had believed. Perhaps of them all, Emmett Chubb was the nearest to correct in his estimation of Levitt's character.

There was small chance he would ever allow any group below to escape the valley to talk and repeat what they knew over too many glasses of whiskey. He was thorough, and he would be thorough enough, and hard enough, to carry out what he had started.

Yet there was little Haney could do until Levitt's next move was revealed. Reynolds and Pogue were gone and the Ruby Hills country lay in the big man's palm. Haney longed for a talk with Scott, for the old storekeeper was a shrewd judge of men, and he listened much and heard everything.

Returning to the fire, he joined Burt and Mabry in eating a quick breakfast. "Now," he said as he finished his last cup of coffee, "we'll see what you've got to show us. Then Mabry an' me will go down into the lava an' push out some more cows. We've got to keep Levitt sweatin'."

Burt, whose leg was rapidly returning to normal, led them through the aspens to the open mesa, and then along its top toward the jumbled maze of boulders that blocked off any approach from the northwest except by the narrow trail Haney used in coming and going.

The way Burt took followed a dim pathway into the boulders and ended at a great leaning slab of granite under which there was a dark, chill-looking opening.

"Come on," he said. "We're going down here!" He had brought with him several bits of candle, and now he passed one to each of them. They stooped, and crept into the hole. The air felt damp inside, and there was a vast, cavernous feeling as of a dark, empty space. Holding their candles high, they saw they were on a steep floor that led away ahead of them, going down and down into an abysmal darkness from which came the faint sound of falling water.

Burt hobbled along ahead of them, and they had descended seventy or eighty feet below the level of the mesa above, when he paused on the rim of a black hole. Leaning forward, Ross Haney saw a bottomless blackness from which there came at intervals a strange sighing, and then a low rumble.

"We got maybe ten minutes, the way I figure it," Burt said. "And then to be on the safe side, we've got to get out." He knelt and touched the rock at the edge of the hole. "Look how smooth. Water done that, water falling on it for years and years. I tried to time it yesterday, an' it seems to come about every three hours. Pressure must build away down inside the mountain somehow, an' then she blows a cork an' water comes a spoutin' an' a spumin' out of this hole. She shoots cl'ar up, nigh to the roof, and she keeps a spoutin' for maybe three, four minutes. Then it dies away, an' that's the end."

"Well, I'm dog-goned!" Mabry exclaimed. "I've heard about this place. Injuns used to call it the Talkin' Mountain. Heard the Navajos speak of it afore I ever came over here."

"Stones come up on that water, too, an' water fills this whole room, just boilin' an' roarin', but that ain't all. Look up there!" He stepped back and pointed, and, moving away from the rim, they looked up.

High above them, in the vaulted top of the cave were several ragged holes. "Back in the trees, too! A man could walk right into them if he wasn't careful, an' he'd go right on through into that, or else break a leg an' lie on the rim until the water came."

"Ugly-lookin'," Ross said. "Let's get out of here."

They turned and started out, and then from behind them came a dull, mounting rumble!

"Run!" Burt's face was suddenly panic-stricken. "Here it comes!"

He lunged forward and, scrambling, fell full length on the steep trail. Haney stooped and grabbed the man, but he was a big man and powerful, and unless Bill Mabry had not grabbed the other arm he never would have gotten him up the steep hole in time.

They scrambled out into the sunlight, their faces pale, and below and behind them they heard the pound and rumble of boulders and the roar of water tumbling in the vast and empty cavern.

"That," Mabry said dryly, "is a good place to keep out of!"

When they returned to the camp, Burt started for his horse. "I'll saddle up," he said, "an' help you *hombres*. I've been loafin' long enough."

"You stay here." Ross turned around and grinned at him. "You keep an eye on the springs, as I've a hunch we'll have more visitors. This is a two-man job. Tomorrow, if we need help, you can go an' we'll leave Bill behind, or I'll stay."

Mabry had little to say on the ride into the lava

beds, but Haney was just as pleased for his thoughts were busy with Sherry and the situation in the valley and at Soledad. He made up his mind he would take a chance and slip into town. Then he could talk to Scott or Kinney, and would be able to find out just what was taking place.

He had no idea what had happened beyond the few words he could catch from the conversation of the posse searching for him, but Scott would know all that had happened. On second thought, it would be wiser to see only Scott, for the chances were that Kinney would be watched. Already the connection with him would be formed in Star Levitt's mind.

The work in the lava beds was hot and tiring. The wild cattle fought like devils and branding them was a slow task and a hazardous one for the two men. Yet by nightfall they had branded enough of them to warrant their work. They camped at night in the cañon, and the following morning started the cattle out through the deep crevasse toward open range. Once they had them started toward Thousand Springs, they returned to the mesa where Rolly was waiting for them.

"Took a ride in last night," he volunteered, "been goin' stale layin' around. I talked to Kinney a little, but they're watchin' him."

"What's happened?" Haney's irritation at Burt's gamble was lost in his eagerness for news.

"Well, Levitt seems to be havin' everythin' his

159

own way. He made Emmett Chubb sheriff, and says it's goin' to be necessary to be strict until they rid themselves of the lawless elements, which probably means us. I talked to Scott, an' he sure wants to see you. Sherry Vernon ain't been seen in town since the fight, an' Bob only oncet, an' then he came an' hightailed it out of there. Levitt, he sent for outside law."

"He did what?"

"Sent for some outside law. He says he aims to have this Reynolds an' Pogue feud cleared up, an' he wants you caught. Says you're a rustler, an' may have had more than a little hand in the killin' at the stock pens. He wants the blame fixed, he says. Also, the story's around"—Burt cleared his throat and avoided Haney's eyes— "that there will be a weddin' out at the VV pretty soon."

Ross stared at the fire. So that was it? Now he would marry Sherry Vernon and the VV would be his in name as well as in appearances, for once they were married he would know how to handle Bob. If Haney was to do anything, it must be done soon. It must be done now.

"Howsoever, there seems to be some talk around. Syd Berdue ain't happy with the new set-up. Kerb Dahl is foreman at the VV, an' Chubb is sheriff. Bob Streeter is foreman on the RR, an' they say Berdue fair raised mischief over that, but Levitt told him he would be taken care of."

"I reckon that's what he's scared of," Mabry said dryly. "I know what I'd do if Star Levitt said I was to be taken care of. I'd either get me a shot at Star or a fast horse out of the country."

"Well, Berdue ain't leavin'. Not willin', anyway. I reckon Star is anxious to have everything looking shipshape for the law when it comes up. They'll be glad to get shut of the trouble anyway, an', if things look pretty, they'll leave them as they be."

Ross pondered the news. Certainly Levitt's position was good. He was a smooth-talking man with a good outward appearance, and, if everything looked settled and calm, the outsiders would go away. The valley would be safely in Levitt's hands, and Ross Haney would be declared an outlaw and hunted by the forces of the law wherever he happened to appear.

It was, apparently, time to come off the mesa and enter the game once more. Suddenly he knew just exactly what he was going to do!

"Somethin' else," Burt added, "there's a lot of talk around about those steers of yours. Seems to be a lot of difference of view as to where they come from. No other brands on 'em, but full-growed steers. There's a rumor around that you've had a herd in the hills for some time."

"Bill," Ross said thoughtfully, "there's been some talk about another man on the VV spread. And when I was out there, I saw a small cabin off across the wash. You know anything about that?"

"No, I don't know anything at all. There's somethin' mighty peculiar about that cabin, an' none of us ever went near it but Star or Kerb Dahl."

Mabry leaned back against a tree and built a smoke. "Dahl, he acted mighty skittish around that cabin, his own self."

When morning came again to the Ruby Hills, Ross Haney mounted the Appaloosa and started by a winding route toward Soledad. He had no intention of getting there before dark unless it could be managed without being seen. While he was about it, he would investigate that mysterious cabin, and learn once and for all if it had anything to do with Sherry and her attitude toward Levitt.

The trail he was using was the same used on the previous trips, a trail that lay along a concealed route through the timber, mountain, and chaparral. It was the trail of which he had learned from the same source as provided the story of the cattle, the lava beds, and the mesa. This might well be the last time he would travel it for he needed no additional warning to let him know that every man's hand would be against him in Soledad.

His own position in the valley was a good one, but must be backed by gun power, and he could not match Levitt as to numbers. However, Levitt himself was bringing the law in, and the law outweighed the brute force of any outlaw or the tricks of any criminal working beyond it.

XIV

Circling around Soledad, he cut down through the chaparral to a position on the point of the ragged hills that overlooked the VV. Then, glass in hand, he took a comfortable position where he could watch all movement on the ranch and began a systematic survey of the entire area below.

The isolated cabin he located without trouble. He studied it for a long time, watching for any evidence of life, but found none. The cabin looked bare and lonely, and no smoke came from its small chimney, nor did anyone approach it. Obviously the cabin held something or someone of great importance to Levitt or it would not be kept so secret.

After a careful survey of the ranch buildings, he decided the door of the cabin was not actually in view of the ranch house, for that view was cut off by the stable and several large stacks of hay for feeding saddle stock through the winter months.

Kerb Dahl was loitering around the ranch yard and he was wearing two guns, but no one else was in view. Once, as dusk drew nearer, he saw Bob Vernon come to the door of the house and stare off toward town, but he turned then without coming outside, and walked back. But in that moment when he had stood in the door, Dahl had walked hastily forward and stood facing him, for all the world like a prison guard.

The evening faded and the stars came out. From away on the desert a soft wind picked up and began to blow gently. Back over the mountains lay a dark curtain of cloud, black and somber. As he glanced that way, Haney saw its bulging billows darting with sudden lightning, and once, like the whimper of far-off trumpets, he heard the distant sound of thunder.

He waited there, his ears attuned to every sound, his eyes roving over the ranch and all its approaches. In what he saw and heard now his life might depend, for in a matter of minutes he was going down there. Yet, aside from the restless roving of Kerb Dahl, there was no evidence of life about the ranch until a light came on. And when that light brightened the windows, Ross got to his feet, brushed the sand from his clothes, and stretched.

Then, leading his horse, he came off the hill, concealed from the ranch by the point of the ridge on which he had waited. He took a winding route up a sandy wash toward the ranch, stopping from time to time to listen once more, then moving on. In the shadows back of the stable, he let the horse stand, reins trailing, with a light touch on the shoulder and a whisper of warning. Nothing now but Haney's own shrill whistle would move him from the spot.

Loosening his guns in their holsters, Ross Haney took a deep breath and turned his eyes on the lonely cabin. Then he went down into the gully and started for the cabin door.

Stark and alone on the knoll it stood, a gloomy little building that seemed somehow ominous and strange. Nearby, he crouched in the darkness listening for any sound of movement that might warn him of a possible occupant. Wind whispered around the eaves and from the ranch house itself there came a rattle of dishes, the sound made plain by that cool night air. Here at the cabin all was silence. The only window was covered with a fragment of sacking, so after a long minute he moved to the door.

His heart pounded against his ribs, and his mouth felt dry. He paused, flattened against the building, and listened once more. Only the wind made a sound to be heard, a soft soughing that seemed to whisper of the impending rain. The clouds towered in the sky now, higher and closer, and the rumble of thunder was close, like a lonely lion, growling in his chest as he paced his cage.

Carefully his hand went to the knob. In the

darkness the metal seemed strangely chill. His right hand moved back to his gun butt, and then, ever so carefully, he turned the knob.

It was locked.

Gently he released the knob. The pause irritated him. He had built himself to a crisis that was frustration in this most obvious of ways, and the piling up of suspense made him reckless. A glance toward the ranch assured him he was unobserved, and probably could not be seen against the blackness along the cabin wall.

This was a puzzle he must solve, and now was the time. There might never be another. Behind the locked door might lie the answer to the mystery, and he moved forward suddenly, and placed his shoulder against the flimsy panel. Light streamed from the bunkhouse windows, too. From the ranch there came only the continuing rattle of dishes, and once a loud splash as someone threw water out onto the ground. Taking the knob in his hand, he turned it, and then putting his shoulder to the door and digging his feet into the earth, he began to push.

The construction was flimsy enough. Evidently whatever was kept there was guarded by Dahl or his partner. Haney relaxed, took in a deep breath, and then putting his shoulder to the door again, he shoved hard. Something cracked sharply, and he drew back, hand on his gun, waiting and listening.

From within there came no sound. From the ranch, all was normal. He put his shoulder again to the door and heaved, but this time the damage had been done and the door came open so suddenly that he sprawled on hands and knees inside!

Cat-like, he wheeled, back to the door and gun in hand. His eyes wide for the darkness, he stared about. The light wind caught the sacking with a ghostly hand and stirred it faintly. Lightning flashed, and the room lay bare before him for an instant.

A wooden chair on its side, a worn table with an empty basin, a cot covered with odorous blankets, and against the wall several stacks of boxes.

Puzzled, Haney crossed to them. They were not heavy. He hesitated to risk the screech of a drawn nail, but by this time he was almost beyond caring. With his fingers, he got a grip on one of the boards that made up the box, and pulled hard. It held, and then, as he strained, it came loose. If it made any sound, it was lost in the convenient rumble of thunder.

Inside the box there was more sacking, and, when that was parted, several round cans, slightly larger and not unlike a snuff can. Lifting one to his nostrils, he sniffed curiously, and from the box came a strange, pungent, half-forgotten odor.

So that's it! he thought. Then he scowled into

the darkness. It did not clarify the position of Sherry, or her brother. And yet, his heart seemed to go empty within him—maybe it did!

Pocketing several of the boxes, he replaced the boards as well as he could and turned the box so as to conceal the more obvious damage. Then he slipped outside and pulled the door to behind him.

Confused by the unexpected turn of events, he returned to his horse, whispered reassuringly, and then went around the stable toward the house.

Nearby was a window, and he moved up under the trees and looked through into what was the dining room of the ranch house. Three people sat at the table. Bob and Sherry Vernon, and, at the head of the table, Star Levitt.

The window was slightly open, and he could hear their voices. Levitt was speaking: "Yes, I think that's the only solution, my dear." His tone was suave, cruel, but decisive. "We shall be married in this house on Monday. You understand?"

"You can't get away with this!" Bob burst out angrily, but the undercurrent of hopelessness in his voice was plain. "It's a devil of a thing! Sherry hates you! What sort of a mind can you have?"

"Sherry will change." Levitt smiled across the table at her. "I promise you both, she will change. Also, it will be convenient for her to be my wife. She cannot testify against me, and I scarcely believe that with her as my wife you'll care to bring any charges, Bob. Also, I'll have control of this ranch, and, as the others are in my hands, the situation is excellent."

"I've a good notion to . . . !" Bob's voice trailed off into sullenness.

"Have you?" Levitt glanced up, his eyes ugly. "Listen, Vernon! Don't give me any trouble! You're in this deeper than I am! You've got murder against you, as well as smuggling. If I'm ever exposed, you know that you and Sherry will both go down with me. What will your precious father think then, with his fine family pride and his bad heart?"

"Shut up!" Bob cried angrily. He leaped to his feet. "If it weren't for Dad, I'd kill you with my bare hands!"

"Really, Bob," Sherry said quietly, "perhaps we should talk this over. I'm not so sure that prison for both of us wouldn't be preferable to being married to Star."

Levitt's face went white and dangerous. "You're flattering," he said dryly, striving to retain his composure. "What, if I may ask, would have happened to Bob if I hadn't gotten him away from that mess and brought him here? The killing of Clyde Aubury was not any ordinary killing."

Aubury? Ross Haney's brows drew together, and he strained his ears to hear more.

"Yes, I think I should have earned your gratitude," Levitt continued. "Instead, I find you falling for that drifting cowhand."

Sherry Vernon's eyes lifted from her plate. "Star," she said coolly, "you could never understand through that vast ego of yours that Ross Haney is several times the man you could ever have been, even if you hadn't become a thief and a blackmailer of women."

Haney's heart leaped, and his lips tightened. In that instant, he would cheerfully have gone through the window, glass and all, and given his life if it would have helped. Yet even in his elation at her praise of him, he could not but admire the coolness and composure. Her manner was quiet, poised. He stared into the window, his heart pounding. Then she lifted her eyes and looked straight into his!

For an instant that seemed an eternity, their eyes held. In hers he saw hope leap into being, then saw her eyes suddenly masked, and she turned her head, passing something to her brother with an idle comment that ignored Levitt completely.

"Well," she said after a minute, her voice sounding just a tone louder, "everything is all right for the time. At least I have until Monday!"

He drew back. That message was for him, and between now and Monday was a lifetime—three whole days! Three days in which many things might be done, in which she might be taken from here—in which he might even kill Star Levitt. For he knew now that was what he would do if the worse came to the worst. He had never yet actually hunted a man down for the purpose of killing him, but he knew that was just what he would do if there was no other way out.

Tiptoeing to the corner of the house, Ross started for the stable and his horse, and then, as he stepped past the last tree, a huge cottonwood, a man stepped out. "Say, you got a match?"

It was Kerb Dahl!

Recognition came to them at the same instant, and the man let out a startled yelp and grabbed for his gun.

There was no time to grapple with the man, no chance for a quick, soundless battle. Too much space intervened so there was only one chance. Even as Dahl's hand grasped his gun, Haney plucked out his own gun and fired.

Flame stabbed from the muzzle, and then a second stab of fire. Dahl took a hesitant step forward, his gun half out. Then the gun belched flame, shooting a hole through the bottom of the holster, and Dahl toppled forward on his face.

Behind Dahl the bunkhouse door burst open, and there was a shout from the ranch house itself. As quickly Ross ducked around the stable and hit the saddle running.

The Appaloosa knew an emergency when he

felt one and he lit out, running like a scared rabbit. A gun barked, then another, but nothing in that part of the country could catch the Appaloosa when he started going places in a hurry, and that was just what he was doing.

On the outskirts of Soledad, with the pounding hoofs of the pursuit far behind, Haney leaped the horse over a gully and took to the desert, weaving a pattern of tangled tracks into a trail where cattle had been driven, then cutting back into the scattered back alleys of Soledad, leaving town a few minutes later, crossing a shale slide and swinging around a butte to hit his old trail for Thousand Springs Mesa.

"Río, you saved my neck tonight, an' we took a scalp. I'd as soon never take another, but if we have to, let 'em all be *hombres* like Dahl."

Yet what was all this about a murder charge against Bob Vernon? And what was their connection with the smuggling and the cans of opium he had found in the cabin? He had known the smell the instant he lifted the can to his nostrils, for it is a smell one does not soon forget. He remembered it from a visit, a few years before, to some of the dives along the Barbary Coast. And now he must think. Somehow, some way, he must free Sherry from this entanglement, and as a last resort he would do it, if he must, by facing Star Levitt with a gun.

XV

Haney's course was clear. Whatever other plans he might have had must be shelved and the whole situation brought into the open by Monday. Studying the situation carefully, he could see little hope, unless the sheriff and the investigating officers from the outside arrived on Monday. Then, if he could present his case—but Levitt would take every measure to avoid that and his only chance would be to get into town before time.

On Sunday night, in absolute blackness, the three rode down the back trail toward Soledad. Outside of town they slackened pace. Ross turned in his saddle as Burt and Mabry came up beside him.

He gestured toward the town. "It looks quiet enough. I'm going to leave my horse at May's. You two leave your horses there, too. Put them in the stable. Then you two hide out in the stable. I'm going first. You follow in a few minutes. I want to see Scott, and he'll go to Allan for me. If the worse comes to the worst, and there is no other way, I'm going gunning for Star. I'd rather die myself than see that girl forced to marry him, or to see him win after all this murder and deceit. However, I may give myself up when the sheriff gets here."

Mabry nodded thoughtfully. "Who are these *hombres* Levitt's bringin' in, Ross? Are they really the law?"

"Yeah, you see he calls Chubb the sheriff. Actually he's only a town marshal. The county seat is over a hundred miles away by trail, an' there's no deputy up here. Star Levitt is shrewd. He knows that sooner or later some word of this scrap will get out. Somebody, on a stage or somewhere, will talk. The chances are they already have. Well, so he sends to the governor for an investigating officer, wanting the whole thing cleared up. That puts him on the map as a responsible citizen. He'll do the talking and the men he selects will back him up, and the whole situation will be smoothed over. The chances are one of his men will be made a deputy sheriff. Then the investigatin' officers will go back to the capital and Levitt's in a nice spot. If any trouble comes up, they will always remember him, apparently rich, a stable citizen, a man who called on the law. They wouldn't believe a thing against him. His skirts will be clear, an' we three will be outlawed. Somehow, we've got to block that an' expose the true state of affairs."

"What is this joker you said you had?" Mabry asked.

"Wait. That will do for the showdown. Nobody knows about that but myself an' Scott. We'll have this whole show well sewed up."

He was the first to move forward, walking the Appaloosa through the encircling trees to May Ashton's cabin on the edge of Soledad. There was no one in sight, but a light glowed in the cabin. He moved up and led his horse into the stable and left it there. Then he slipped along the wall of the house until he could glance into a window. The waitress was inside, and alone.

She opened the door at his tap, and he slipped inside. "You!" she gasped. "We were wondering how to get word to you. Star Levitt is marrying Sherry tomorrow."

"I know. What about the officers from the capital?"

"They'll be in tomorrow, too. In the morning. The sheriff is coming up from the county seat, and some attorney from the capital named Ward Clymer. Two state Rangers are coming with them. I've heard it all discussed in the restaurant."

"They will have a hearing? Where?"

"In the lobby of the hotel. It's the only place large enough, aside from the Bit and Bridle. I heard Voyle talking with Syd Berdue about it. Incidentally," she added quickly, "there's a warrant out for your arrest. Emmett Chubb has it. They want you for killing Kerb Dahl. Was that you?"

"Uhn-huh, but it was a fair shake. In fact, he went for his gun first. I had no choice but to shoot."

"Well, the order is out to shoot on sight, and they have Reward posters ready to go out tomorrow morning. They will be all over town for the officers to see when they come in. You're wanted for murder, dead or alive, and they are offering a thousand dollars."

Ross smiled wryly. "That will make it worse! A thousand dollars is money enough to start the blood hunters out. Now, listen. I'm going to Scott, and I'm going now. Mabry and Burt will be in soon, and they'll hide here in the stable. They will be standing by in case of emergency. I'll try to communicate with you in case of really serious trouble, and then you can get word to them. I intend to give myself up to the officials and make them hold a preliminary hearing right here. I can talk them into that, I think. Then we can get facts in front of them."

"Ross, don't plan on anybody siding you," May said quickly. "Chubb has been around town with Hanson, and they have frightened everybody. You can't depend on a soul. I don't even know whether I'd have nerve enough to back you up, but I'm afraid Allan will. He's that kind."

The street was dark when Ross Haney stepped out of May's cabin. He did not try to keep out of sight, realizing that such an attempt, if seen, would be even more suspicious. He walked rapidly down the street, staying in the deep shadows, but walking briskly along. Scott was the man he must see. He must get to him at once, and he would know what to do. Also, it would be a place to hide.

Glancing across the street, he saw a half dozen horses standing at the hitch rail in front of the Bit and Bridle. There was light flooding from the windows, and the sound of loud laughter from within.

A man opened the door and stumbled drunkenly into the street, and for a moment Ross hesitated, feeling uneasy. The street was altogether too quiet; there was too little movement. He turned at right angles and went between a couple of buildings, starting for the back door of Scott's place. Once he thought he glimpsed a movement in the shadows, and hesitated, but, after watching and seeing nothing more, he went on up to the back door and tapped gently. The door opened, and he stepped in.

Scott glanced at him, and alarm sprang into his eyes.

"Set down," he said. "Set down. You've sure been stirrin' up a pile of trouble, Haney."

He poured a cup of coffee and placed it on the table. "Drink that," he said quietly. "It will do you good."

Scott stared at him as he lifted the cup. "Big trouble's goin' to break loose, Scott," Haney said. "I hope I can handle it."

His ears caught a subtle whisper of movement

outside, and his eyes lifted, then his face went to a dead, sickly white.

Scott had a shotgun, and its twin barrels were pointed right at his stomach.

"Sit tight, son," he said sternly. "A move an' I'll cut you in two." He lifted his voice. "All right, out there! Come on in! I've got him!"

The door burst open and Emmett Chubb sprang into the room, and with him was Voyle, Tolman, and Allan Kinney!

Chubb's eyes gleamed and his pistol lifted. "Well, Mister Ross Haney, who's top dog now?"

"Hold it!" Scott's shotgun made a sharp movement. "You take her easy, Emmett Chubb! This man's my prisoner. I'm claimin' the reward, right now. Moreover, I'm holdin' him alive for Levitt!"

"You will not!" Chubb snarled. "I'll kill the dirty dog!"

"Not unless you want a blast from this shotgun!" Scott snapped. The old outlaw's blue eyes sparked. "Nobody's beatin' me out of my money! Kinney, here, he has a finger in it, maybe, because he tipped me off, but you take him away from me over my dead body!"

Baffled, Chubb stared from one to the other.

"He's right, Emmett," Kinney agreed. "He got him first."

Ross Haney stood flat-footed, staring from Kinney to Scott. "Sold out!" he sneered. "I might have suspected it!"

Kinney flushed, but Scott shrugged.

"A thousand dollars is a lot of money, boy. I've seen men killed for a sight less."

"Let's take him off to jail, then," Chubb said. "This ain't no place for him."

"He stays right here," Scott said harshly. "He's my prisoner until Levitt gets him, an' then Levitt can do what he's a mind to. Nobody's beatin' me out o' that money. Stay here an' help guard if you want, but don't you forget for one minute that he's my prisoner. This shotgun won't forget it."

Kinney slipped around behind Haney and lifted his guns. Reluctantly Haney backed into a corner and was tied to a chair. Shocked by the sudden betrayal, he could only stare from Allan to Scott, appalled by the sudden turn of fortune.

From the high, if desperate hopes of the day, he was suddenly smashed back into hopelessness, a prisoner, betrayed by the men he had most confidence in. How could they have known he was in town? There was only one way. May must have betrayed him! She and Allan must have planned together, and, when he left her house, she must have gotten word to him at once.

Chubb dropped into a chair and pulled one of his guns over into his lap. "I'd like to blast his heart out," he said sullenly. "What you frettin' so about, Scott? You get the money, dead or alive."

"Sure," Scott said. "And if you kill him, you'll lay claim to it. I wouldn't trust you across the

179

street where that much money was concerned. Nor any of you." He chuckled, his eyes sneering at Haney. "Anyway, Levitt's top dog around here from now on, an' he's the boy I do business with. I'm too old to be shoved out in the cold at my time of life. I ain't figurin' on it. I'll work with Star, an' he'll work with me."

"I never heard of you bein' so thick with him." Chubb's irritation was obvious.

Scott chuckled. "Who got him into this country, do you suppose? I've knowed him for years! Who told him this place was right for a smart man? I did! That's who! Haney, here, he figured on the same thing. He figured on takin' over when Reynolds an' Pogue were out of it, but he was leavin' too much to chance. Star doesn't leave anything to chance."

Bitterly Ross Haney stared at the floor. This time he was finished. If Mabry and Burt had gone to May's, they would have been sold out, too. He listened, straining his ears for shots, hoping at least one of them would manage to fight it out and go down with a gun in his hand.

The situation was all Levitt's now. The man was a front rider, and these others were with him. He stared at Kinney, and the young man's eyes wavered and looked away. How could he have guessed that such a man would sell him out? And Scott? Of course, the old man was an admitted outlaw, or had been. Still, he had felt very close to the old man, and liked him very much.

There was no chance for Sherry now—unless. . . . His eyes narrowed with thought. What would they do with him? Would they get word to Star that he was a prisoner, then smuggle him out of town to be killed? Or would they bring him out in the open with evidence arrayed against him, or kill him trying to escape?

If only there would be some break, some chance to talk to Ward Clymer or the sheriff! Of course, held as a prisoner, with Reward posters out and stories Star and his men would tell, he would have himself in a bad position even before they talked to him, for they would be prejudiced against him, and everything he might say. And what evidence had he? Star Levitt would have plenty, and, as May had told him, no one in town would testify for him against Star. They were frightened, or they were getting on the band-wagon. He was through.

Unless—there was a vague hope—that Mabry and Burt had not been captured. If they could somehow free him? Knowing the manner of men they were, he knew they would not hesitate to make the attempt.

XVI

In the back room of the store the night slid slowly by and crawled into the gray of day, slowly, reluctantly. The rising sun found the sky overcast and no opening in the clouds through which it could shine down on the clustered, false-fronted frame buildings and adobes of Soledad. A lone Mexican, a burro piled twice its own height with sticks, wandered sleepily down the town's dusty street.

Pat walked out of the Bit and Bridle and stared at the sky, then turned and walked back within. A pump rattled somewhere, then began a rhythmical speaking.

Half asleep in his bonds, Ross Haney heard the water gushing into the pail in spouts of sound. He stirred restlessly, and his chair creaked. He opened his eyes to see four pairs of eyes leveled at him. Emmett Chubb, Voyle, Allan Kinney, and Scott all sat, ready and watchful. His lids fluttered and closed. Behind them his mind began to plan, to contrive.

No man is so desperate as a prisoner. No man so ready to plan, to try to think his way out. If only his hands were free! In a few minutes, an hour at most, the stage would rattle down the street and halt in front of the Cattleman's Rest Hotel and the passengers would go into the restaurant to eat. Later they might go upstairs to sleep. During that interval, he would know his fate. He touched a tongue to dry lips.

"Al," Scott said suddenly, "you take this here shotgun. I'll throw together a few ham an' eggs. I'm hungry as a hibernatin' bear in the springtime."

Tolman, who had left earlier, returned now and stuck his head in the door. "Stage a-comin'!" he said. "An' Syd Berdue just blowed in!"

"That VV bunch in yet?" Chubb asked, without turning his head. "When Dolph Turner gets in, you tell him about this. He'll see that Levitt knows first of all."

Scott was working around the stove and soon the room was filled with the pleasant breakfast smell of frying ham and eggs and the smell of coffee. Despite his worry, Haney realized he had been hungry, and for the first time recalled he had eaten nothing the night before.

Emmett Chubb got up. He was a stocky, swarthy man with a square jaw and a stubble of beard. His hair was unkempt, and, when he crossed the room to splash water on his face and hands, Ross noted his worn guns had notches carved in them, three on one gun, five on the other. Eight men.

"The only thing I'm sorry for," Chubb said as he dried his hands, his eyes on Haney, "is that I didn't get the chance to shoot it out with you in the street." His black eyes were sneering and cold. "I'd like to put you in the dust," he said. "I'd like to see you die."

"Well," Haney said dryly, "my hands are tied, so you're safe enough to try. You're a lot of yellow-backed double-crossers. You, Chubb, are a cheap murderer. You blew town fast enough after killin' Vin Carter or you'd have had a chance to draw on me . . . or run."

Chubb walked across the room and stopped, his feet apart, in front of Haney. Lifting his open palm, he slapped Ross three times across the mouth. Scott did not turn, and Kinney shuffled his feet on the floor.

"Maybe Levitt will give me the job," he said harshly. "I hope he does."

The door opened suddenly and three men stood there. Ross Haney's head jerked up as he saw Levitt. Star Levitt glanced from Chubb to Scott, and then indicated the men with him.

"Neal an' Baker, of the Rangers. They want the prisoner."

Chubb stared, disappointment and resentment struggling for place in his eyes. "Here he is. Scott's been holdin' him."

Neal bent over Haney and cut the ropes that tied his arms. "You come with us. We're havin' the hearin' right now."

Haney turned, and, as he started toward the door, he saw Scott smiling. The old outlaw looked right into his eyes and winked, deliberately. What did that mean?

Scowling, Haney walked across the street toward the hotel. Neal glanced at him a couple of times. "You know a man named Mabry?"

"Bill Mabry?" Ross turned to Neal, astonished. "Why, sure. He works for me, an' a mighty good man."

"When Clymer asks you questions," Neal said, "give him the information you have straight, honest, and without prejudice."

Puzzled by the suggestion, Ross Haney walked into the room, and was shown to a chair.

A big man with a capable, shrewd-looking face glanced at him sharply, then went back to examining some documents on the table. Several other men trooped in, and then Sherry and Bob Vernon walked into the room. More and more astonished, Ross stared from one to the other, trying to see what must have happened.

He had never believed that Levitt would allow Clymer to confront the Vernons, or himself, if it could be avoided. Yet here they all were, and it looked like a showdown. Allan Kinney was there, and May. The pretty waitress glanced at him, and he averted his eyes. Scott had come over, and Star Levitt was one of the last to come into the room.

From the dark expression on Levitt's face, he decided all could not be going well for the big man, and the thought cheered him. Anything that was bad news for Levitt was sure to be good news for him.

Ward Clymer sat back in his chair and looked over the room, his eyes noncommittal. "Now, friends," he said briskly, "this is an entirely informal hearing to try to clarify the events leading up to the battle between the Reynolds and Pogue factions and to ascertain the guilt, if any, of those who are here with us. Also," he glanced at Haney, "I am informed that Ross Haney, the cattleman, is held on a charge of murder for the slaying of one Kerb Dahl, a cowhand from the VV. If such is the truth, and if the evidence warrants it, Ross Haney will be taken south to the county seat for trial. In the meantime, let us examine the evidence.

"Mister Levitt, will you tell us the events that preceded the fight between Reynolds and Pogue?"

Star Levitt got to his feet, very smooth, very polished. He glanced around, smiled a little, and began. "It seems that before I arrived in the Ruby Hills country there had been considerable trouble over water and range rights, with sporadic fighting between the two big outfits. The VV, owned by the Vernons, was not involved in this feud, although there seemed to be some desire on the part of both outfits to possess the VV holdings and water. On the day the fight started there

186

was some minor altercation over branding, and it led to a shooting which quickly spread until most of the hands on both sides were involved, with resulting deaths."

"What was your part in the fight?" Clymer asked shrewdly.

"None at all, sir. I saw trouble coming and withdrew my men and got out of the way myself. After it was over, we did what we could for the wounded."

"There are no witnesses present from the other outfits?"

"Oh, yes! Emmett Chubb, now the town marshal, survived the fight. Also Voyle, of the Box N, is here. Kerb Dahl, of the VV, who was in the middle of things was later murdered by the prisoner, Ross Haney."

"Sir?" Haney asked suddenly.

Clymer's eyes shifted to him, hesitated, and then asked: "Did you have a question?"

"Yes, I'd like to ask Star Levitt where his range holdings were."

"I don't see that the question has any bearing on the matter," Levitt replied coolly.

"It's a fair question," Clymer admitted. "It may have some later bearing on it. I understand you were running cattle. Where was your headquarters?"

Levitt hesitated. "On the VV," he said. "You see I am soon to marry Miss Vernon."

Clymer glanced curiously at Haney. "Does that answer your question?"

"Sure, it answers it for now. Only I want it plain to everybody that Star Levitt had no buildings on the range other than cattle and the use of the VV headquarters."

Levitt stared at Haney, and shrugged in a bored manner. The attorney then asked Chubb and Voyle a few questions about the killing, and through Scott, Pat, the bartender, and others brought out the facts of the long-standing feud between the Reynolds and Pogue outfits. Every story served to bolster Levitt's position. Bob Vernon offered his evidence in short, clipped sentences, and then Sherry hers.

As she started to return to her chair, Haney spoke up. "Another question. Sherry, did anyone warn you away from the roundup, telling you to leave at once, that there might be trouble?"

She hesitated. "Why, yes. Star Levitt did."

"I could see some of the men were spoiling for a fight," Star said quietly. "It seemed a bad place for a woman, due to the impending trouble and the profanity attending the work of the men."

"May I ask a few questions?" Ross asked.

"Mister Clymer," Levitt interrupted, "this man Haney is a troublemaker! His questions can do no good except to try to incriminate others and to put himself in a better light. The man is a murderer!"

Clymer shrugged. "We're here to ascertain the facts. However, the prisoner should be examined in connection with the killing of Kerb Dahl. What have you to say to that, Haney?"

"That it is impossible to divide the killing of Dahl from the other sides of the case. Nor is it going to be of any use to talk of it until the events leading up to that point are made plain."

"Well, that's reasonable enough," Clymer said. "Go ahead."

Levitt's lips tightened and his nostrils flared. Voyle had walked into the back of the room with Syd Berdue, and they stood there, surveying the crowd. With them was the silent man who had been Dahl's partner.

"I want to ask Levitt how many hands he had when he came into this country," Ross said evenly.

Star was puzzled and wary. "Why, not many. What difference does it make?"

"How many? You used the VV spread . . . how many hands did *you* have?"

"Why, one was actually all that came with me." The question puzzled Levitt and disturbed him. He couldn't see where it pointed.

"The one man was that short, dark man at the back of the room, wasn't it? The man called Turner?"

"That's right."

Haney turned suddenly in his chair and fired

the question at Dahl's partner. "Turner, what's a piggin' string?"

"What?" The man looked puzzled and frightened. The question startled him, and he was irritated at being suddenly noticed.

"I asked what a piggin' string was. I'd also like to know what a grulla is."

Turner turned his head from side to side, eager for a way out, but there was none. He wet his lips with his tongue, and swallowed. "I don't know," he said.

"These questions make no sense at all!" Levitt said irritably. "Let's get on with the murder hearing!"

"They make sense to me," Ross replied. Then turning to Clymer, he added: "You, sir, were raised on a cow ranch, so you know that a piggin' string is a short piece of rope used to tie a critter when it's throwed . . . thrown. You also know that a grulla is a mouse color, a sort of gray, an' usually applied to horses. The point I'm gettin' at is that Levitt came into this country with one man who wasn't a cowhand. Turner doesn't know the first thing about a ranch or about cattle."

"What's that got to do with it?" Levitt demanded.

Clymer was looking at Ross Haney thoughtfully. He began to smile as he anticipated the reply.

"Why, just this, Levitt. How many cattle did you bring into this country?" Haney demanded sharply. He leaned forward. "An' how many have you got now?"

Somebody out in the room grunted and Scott was grinning from ear to ear. The question had caught Levitt flat-footed. Clymer turned on him, his eyes bright with interest. "A good question, Mister Levitt. On the way here you told me you ran a thousand head. Where did you get them?"

"That's got nothing to do with it!" Levitt shouted angrily. For the first time he was out in the open, and Ross Haney had led him there, led him by the nose into a trap. As Haney knew, when pushed, Levitt grew angry, and it was that he was playing for.

"Mister Clymer," Ross interrupted, "I think it has a lot to do with it. This man, claimin' to be a representative rancher, admits comin' into this country with one man who wasn't a cowhand even if he may be fairly good with a gun. No two men like that are bringin' in a thousand head of cattle into this country an' brandin' 'em. But I'll show you that Levitt does have a thousand head, or near to it, an' every one with a worked-over brand!"

"That's a lie!" Levitt shouted, leaping to his feet.

Ross settled back in his chair, smiling. "Now ask me about the killin' of Kerb Dahl," he said gently.

Star Levitt sagged back in his chair, flushed and angry. He had let go of his temper. Despite his burning rage, he knew he was in an ugly position where Haney, by his fool questions, had led him. The killing led away from the cattle, so he decided to jump at the chance.

Before he could speak, however, Clymer asked Haney: "If he has the branded cattle now, who branded them?"

"Kerb Dahl, the man I killed on the VV, Voyle of the Box N, Tolman, who hired on after Levitt got here, an' Emmett Chubb, among others."

"That's absurd!" Levitt said contemptuously.

"Sherry, name the men you heard talking at Thousand Springs," Ross asked quickly.

The sudden question startled her, and, before Levitt could catch her eye, she glanced up and replied: "Why, Dahl was there, and Voyle, Tolman, and Sydney Berdue."

"What did they talk about?"

Levitt was leaning forward in his chair, his eyes upon her. Sherry glanced at him, and her eyes wavered. "Why, I. . . ." Her voice trailed off.

"Before you answer," Ross told her, "let me tell you that you've been the victims, you and your brother, of the foulest trick ever played." Haney turned to Clymer: "Sir, Miss Vernon was concealed near the springs and overheard some of the plotting between the men mentioned. These were the same men who altered the brands for Levitt. Through them Levitt engineered and planned the whole fight, forcing an issue between Reynolds and Pogue deliberately, and in the battle, killing the two men who opposed him in the Ruby Hills country. It will no doubt strike you that among the survivors of that battle were *all* the men seen by Miss Vernon at the springs. Also," he added, "Levitt was blackmailing the Vernons, using their ranch as a storage depot and transfer point for his deals in the opium trade."

XVII

Knocked off balance by these public revelations, Star Levitt struggled to his feet, his face ashen. The carefully planned coup was tumbling about his ears, and he who had come into the valley as a leader in a dope ring, and planned to become the legitimate owner of a great ranch, suddenly saw the whole thing reduced to chaos.

"Furthermore," Ross got to his feet, and the ringing sound of his voice reduced to silence the stir in the room, "I think this is the proper time to make a few points clear." Opening his shirt, he drew a leather wallet from inside it and from the wallet drew a handful of papers that he passed to Clymer. "Will you tell Mister Levitt," he said, "what you have there?"

Clymer glanced at them, then looked up in

193

amazement. "Why, these are deeds!" he exclaimed, glancing from Haney to Levitt. "These indicate that you are the owner of both Hitson Springs and the Bullhorn ranch headquarters, including the water right. Also, here are papers that show Haney has filed on the Thousand Springs area!"

"What?" Star Levitt's fingers gripped the arms of his chair and his brow creased. Before his eyes came the whole plan he had made, all his planning, his actions—all were rendered perfectly futile. Who controlled the water in those three sources controlled the Ruby Hills, and there was no way of circumventing it. From the beginning he had been beaten, and now he had been made ridiculous.

"I told you," Haney said quietly, looking at Levitt, "that you had overlooked the obvious. Somehow a crook always does. Now, sir," Ross said to Clymer, "with the cattle brands I can show you, the evidence we can produce, I'd say that you have a strong case for robbery and murder against Star Levitt!"

There was a slight stir in the back of the room, and Haney's eyes shifted. Emmett Chubb was slipping from the room to the street.

As the accusation rang in the silent room, Star Levitt held himself taut. The crashing of his plans meant less to him now than the fact that he had been shown up for a fool by the cowhand he despised and hated. Suddenly the rage that was building within him burst into a fury that was almost madness. His face went white, his eyes glassy and staring, and, letting out a choking cry, he sprang for Haney.

Warned by Sherry's scream, Ross jerked his eyes back from the vanishing Chubb and lunged from where he stood, swinging two brain-jarring blows to the head. They rocked Levitt, but nothing could stop his insane rush, and Haney gave ground before the onslaught. Levitt swung wildly with both hands, beside himself with hate and fury.

But Ross lunged at him, burying a right in the bigger man's stomach, then hooking a powerful, jarring left to the chin. Levitt staggered and Ross, eager for battle, bulled into him, bringing his head down on Levitt's shoulder and smashing away with both hands in a wicked body attack. He threw the punches with all the power built into his shoulders by years of bulldogging steers and hard range work.

He caught Levitt with a wicked overhand right, and battered him back into the chairs. The crowd scattered. From somewhere outside Ross heard the sharp rap of a shot, and then another. Then quiet. His right smashed Levitt over a chair, and the big man came up with a lunge, grabbing for the chair itself.

Ross rushed him and Star tried to straighten, but

Haney clubbed him with a fist on the kidney and the big man went to his knees. Ross stepped back, panting. "Get up!" he said. "Get up an' take it!"

Levitt lunged to his feet and Ross smashed his lips with a sweeping left. He ripped a gash in Levitt's cheek with a right. Star tottered back, his eyes glazed. He straightened then, shook his head, some measure of cunning returning to him. Suddenly he turned and hurled himself through the glass of the window!

Ross sprang to the window after him, and caught a fleeting glimpse of Emmett Chubb as a bullet whirred within a hair of his cheek and buried itself in the window frame. There was a clatter of horses' hoofs, then silence.

Haney's hands fell helplessly. Scott moved up beside him, handing him his guns. "Sorry I couldn't get 'em to you sooner," he said, "but you did plenty without 'em."

Clymer caught his arm. "You've loyal friends, Haney. Burt and Mabry stopped the stage outside of town. Levitt had ridden on ahead, and they took time to tell me a lot of things, and asked that I get you and the Vernons together with Levitt and withhold judgment until you had talked and I had listened. As it happens," he added, "Neal and I had both been reared on ranches where Mabry worked. We knew him for a good man, and an honest one. From the first we had doubts that all Levitt had told us was the truth. Mabry also had a cowhide with him, and any Western man could see the brand had been altered from a VV to Three Diamonds."

Ross shoved his guns into his holsters and pushed his way to Sherry who was standing, white and still, near the door, waiting for him. He said gently: "Sherry, we can talk about it some other time, but I think I can make a rough guess at most of it. Why don't you go in and get some coffee? I'll join you in a minute."

Mabry and Burt were waiting outside, and they had the Appaloosa. "We can chase 'em, boss," Rolly said, "but they've got quite a start."

"Later. I heard some shouting. What was it?"

"That was Voyle," Mabry said grimly. "He made a rush for his horse an' met Rolly halfway. He made a grab for his gun, an' I guess he wasn't as gun slick as he figured."

"Tolman?"

"Roped an' hog-tied. He'll go south with the Rangers, an', unless I miss my guess, he'll talk all the way. We've got Turner, too."

"Incidentally," Mabry added, "don't you jump to no conclusions about Kinney an' Scott. I ain't had much time to talk to Scott, but we moved down to May's like you said, an' all three of us seen you follered to Scott's by some of Levitt's crowd. They had us 'way outnumbered, an' Kinney came up and said if he butted in he might keep you from gettin' killed."

"That was my idea," Scott put in. "I thought I seen somethin' in the shadows when I let you in, an' I knowed I either had to get you as my prisoner or we'd both be in a trap. Chubb would kill you sure as shootin' if he got a chance, but as my prisoner I'd have the right to interfere."

"So, then Levitt, Chubb, an' Berdue are the only ones that got away?" Ross mused.

"Uhn-huh," Mabry agreed, and then, running his fingers through his coarse red hair, he commented: "That ain't good! I know that sort, an' you can take my word for it, they'll be back."

Yet as the days found their way down the year and the summer faded toward autumn, there was no further sign of the three missing men. The mornings became chill, but the sun still lay bright and golden upon the long valley, and the view from the growing house upon the mesa top changed from green to green and gold shot through with streaks of russet and deep red. The aspen leaves began to change and sometimes in the early morning the countryside was white with the touch of frost.

Rumors came occasionally to their ears. There had been a bank held up at Weaver, a stage had been looted and two men killed at Cañon Pass, and one of the three bandits had been recognized by a passenger as Emmett Chubb. Then the town marshal in Pie Town was shot down when he attempted to question a big, handsome man with a beard.

When Sherry rode the ˅
Ruby Hills, Ross Haney
side, and the Appaloosa
stant companions. Des
came of any of the th
Haney was worried

"Ross," Sherry said ˄
ised to take me to the crater.
Why not today?"

He hesitated uneasily. "That place has
faloed," he said after a while. "I never go into
myself without wishing I was safely out. The
way those big rocks hang over the trail scares a
man. If they ever fell while we were in there,
we'd never get out, never in this world."

She smiled. "At least we'd be together."

He grinned, and shoved his hat back with a
quick, familiar gesture. His eyes twinkled. "That
sure would be something, but I'd not like to have
you confined in that place all your life. You
might get tired of me. This way you can see a
few folks once in a while an' maybe I'll wear
better."

"But you've been there so many times, Ross,
and Rolly tells me it's perfectly beautiful. I want
to see the ice caves, too."

Below them there was a faint rumbling and
stirring within the mountain and they exchanged
a glance. "I'm getting used to it now," he
admitted, "but when I first heard it, that rumbling

hills. When we move into the
have those holes fenced off. They
ngerous."

Ever since you took me down there
ed me that awful hole, I've been fright-
it. Suppose someone was trapped down
with a foot caught, or something? It would
rightful."

It would be the end," Ross replied grimly.
When that geyser shoots up there, it brings
rocks with it that weigh fifty or sixty pounds, and
they rattle around in that cave like seeds in a
gourd. You wouldn't have to have a foot caught,
either. All you would have to do would be to get
far enough away from the mouth of that cave so
you couldn't make it in a few steps. A man
wouldn't have a chance."

They were riding down the mesa through the
slender aspens, their graceful white trunks like
slender alabaster columns. The trail was carpeted
with the scarlet and gold of autumn leaves.

"Somehow it all seems like some dreadful
dream," she said suddenly. "We'd been so happy,
Bob and I. It was fun on the ranch, working with
the men, building our own place, learning all the
new things about the West. Bob loved handling
the horses and working with cattle, and then,
when we were happiest, Star Levitt came out to
the ranch. You can't imagine what a shock it was
to us, for we thought all that had been left behind

and forgotten. Our brother, the oldest one in the family, had gone down to Mexico and got mixed up with a girl down there, and started using dope. He'd always been Father's favorite, and we all loved him, but Ralph was always weak and easily led. Levitt got hold of him, and used his name for a front to peddle dope in the States.

"Father has been ill for a long time with a heart condition that became steadily worse. He had just two great prides, two things to live for. One was his family reputation and the other was his children. Principally that meant Ralph. We knew about it, but we kept it from Dad, and later, when Ralph was killed down there, we managed to keep the whole truth of the story from him. We knew the shock and the disgrace would kill him, and, if by some chance he lived, he would feel the shame and the disgrace so much that his last years would be nothing but sorrow.

"Star told us that he needed our ranch. It was the proper working base for him, not too far from Mexico, yet in easy reach of a number of cities. He said he wanted to use the ranch for a head-quarters for two months, and then he would leave. If we did not consent, he threatened to expose the whole disgraceful affair and see that my father heard it all. We were foolish, of course, but it is so hard to know what to do. And Levitt didn't give us time. He just started moving in. The next thing we knew he had his own men on the ranch and we were almost helpless. Reynolds and Pogue were outlaws or as bad, and we could not turn to them. There was nobody, until you came."

Ross nodded grimly. "Don't I know it? When I started digging into the background of this country, I found less good people here than anywhere I ever knew. And the best folks were all little people."

"It was after he had been here a few weeks," Sherry continued, "that he decided to stay. He was shrewd enough to know he couldn't keep on like that forever, and here was a good chance to have power, wealth, and an honest income. He saw the fighting between the Box N and RR was his chance."

The two rode on in silence, their horses' hoofs making little sound on the leaf-covered trail. Suddenly, before Ross realized how they were riding, they were at the entrance to the lava bed trail.

Sherry laughed mischievously. "All right, now. As long as we're here, why don't we go in? We can be back before dark, you told me so yourself."

He shrugged. "All right, have it your own way."

XVIII

Very reluctantly the Appaloosa turned into the narrow trail between the great black rolls of lava. Once started, there was no turning back, for until a rider was well within the great cleft itself, there was insufficient room for any turning of the horses.

When they reached the deepest part of the crevasse, where in some bygone age an earthquake or volcanic eruption had split the rim of the crater deep into the bedrock, Ross pointed out the great crags suspended over the trail.

"This place will be inaccessible someday," he told her. "There will be an earthquake or some kind of a jar, and those rocks will fill the cleft, so there will be no trail or place for one. From the look of them, a man might get them started with a bar or lever of some kind. I never ride in here without getting the creeps at the thought. They are just lying up there, and all they need is the slightest start, and they would come roaring and tumbling down."

Tilting her head back, Sherry could see what he meant, and for the first time she understood something of the fear that Ross had of this place. One enormous slab that must have weighed hundreds of tons seemed to be hanging, ready to slide at the slightest touch. It was an awesome feeling to be riding down here, with no sound but the *click* of their horses' hoofs, and to have those enormous rocks poised above them.

Yet once within the crater itself, she forgot her momentary fears in excitement over the long level of green grass, the running water, and the towering cliffs of the crater that seemed to soar endlessly toward the vast blue vault of the sky. Great clouds piled up in an enormous mass in the east and north, seeming to add their great height to the height of the cliffs.

It was warm and pleasant in the sunlight, and they rode along without talking, listening to the lazy sound of the running water, and watching the movements of the few remaining great red and brindle cattle that were becoming more tame due to the frequency of visits.

Haney said: "There must have been more than six hundred down here, and probably would have been more, but there are a good many varmints around. I've seen cougars down here, an' heard 'em."

"Where are the ice caves?" Sherry demanded. "I want to see them. Rolly was telling me about the crystals."

For two hours they rambled on foot over the great crater and in and out of the caves. They found several where cattle and horses had been drinking, and whatever cattle they found, they started back toward the trail. Then suddenly, as they were about to leave, Sherry caught Haney's arm. "Ross!" There was sudden fear in her voice. "Look!"

It was a boot track, small and quite deep. Her breath caught. "It might be . . . Rolly!" Her voice was tight, her fear mounting.

"No, it wasn't Rolly." Mentally he cursed himself for ever bringing her here. "That foot is smaller than either Mabry's or Burt's, an' a heavy man made it. Let's get out of here."

When they were outside, he could see the pallor of her face in the last of the sunlight. He glanced at the sky, surprised at the sudden shadows although it was drawing on toward evening. Great gray thunderclouds loomed over the crater, piling up in great, bulging, ominous clouds. It was going to rain, and rain hard.

Leading the way, he started for the horses, every sense alert and wary, yet he saw no one. His movements started the cattle drifting again, and, as they reached the horses, he told her, glancing at the sky: "You go ahead. I think I'll start the rest of the cattle out of here while I'm at it."

"You can't do it alone," she protested.

"I'll try. You head for home now. You'll get soaked."

"Nonsense! I have my slicker, and. . . ." Her voice faded and her eyes fastened on something beyond Ross's shoulder, widening with fear and horror.

He knew instantly what it was she saw, and for a fleeting moment he considered making his draw as he turned, but realized the girl was directly in the line of fire.

"And so, after so long a time, we meet again!" The voice was that of Star Levitt. But there was a strange tone in it now, less of self-assurance and something that sounded weirdly like madness, or something akin to it.

Carefully Ross Haney turned and met the eyes that told him the worst. All the neatness and glamour of the man was gone. The white hat was soiled, his shirt was dirty, his face unshaven. His eyes were still the large, magnificent eyes, but now the light of insanity was in them. Haney realized the line between sanity and something less had always been finely drawn in this man. Defeat and frustration had been all that was needed to break that shadow line.

"Oh, this is great!" Levitt chortled. "Today we make a clean sweep! I get you, and later, Sherry! And while I am doing that, Chubb and Berdue will finish off Mabry and Burt. They are up on the mesa now, waiting for them!"

"On the mesa?" Haney shrugged. "They'll never surprise the boys there. Whenever one of us has not been on the mesa all day, we are very careful. We've been watching for you, Levitt."

Star smiled. "Oh, have you? But we found our own hiding place. We found a cave there, an ideal spot, and that's where they'll wait until they can catch Mabry and Burt without warning them."

"A cave?" Ross repeated. Horror welled up within him and he felt the hackles rising along his neck and his scalp prickled at the thought. "A cave? You mean you've been in that cave on the mesa?"

Levitt smiled. "Only to look, enough to know that it was an ideal hiding place. At first, I planned to stay, too, but then, when I saw you two leaving the mesa and heading for the lava beds, I decided this was a better chance. Besides"—he glanced at Sherry—"I want her for a while . . . alone. She needs to be taught a lesson."

Ross Haney stared at him. "Levitt, you're mad. That cave where those men are hiding is a death-trap. If they aren't within a few feet of the opening, they won't have a chance to get out of there alive. Did you see that black hole in the center? That's a geyser. Those men will be trapped and drowned."

Levitt's smile vanished. "That's a lie, of course. If it isn't, it won't matter. I was through with them, anyway. And Mabry and Burt are small fry. It is you two that I wanted."

Ross Haney had shifted his position slightly now and he was facing Levitt. His heart was pounding, for he knew there was only one chance for them. He must draw, and he must take a chance on beating Levitt to the shot. He would be hit, he was almost sure, but regardless of that he must kill Star Levitt.

Wes Hardin had beaten men to the shot several times when actually covered with a gun. There were others who had done it, but he was no fool, and knew how tremendously the odds weighed against him. Thunder rumbled and a few spatters of rain fell.

"Better get your slicker, Sherry," he said calmly. "You'll get wet."

His eyes were riveted upon Star Levitt, but what he waited for happened. As the girl started to move, Levitt's eyes flickered for a fraction of an instant, and Ross Haney went for his gun.

Levitt's gun flamed, but he swung his eyes back and shot too fast, for the bullet ripped by Haney's head just as Ross flipped the hammer of his gun.

Once! Twice! And then he walked in on the bigger man, his heart pounding, Levitt's gun flaming in his face, intent only upon getting in as many shots as possible before he was killed.

A bullet creased his arm and his hand dropped. Awkwardly he fired with his left-hand gun, and knew the shot had missed, yet Star Levitt, his shirt dark with blood, was wilting before his eyes, his body fairly riddled with the bullets from Haney's first, accurate shots.

Ross held his gun carefully, then fired again, and the shot ripped away the bridge of Star's nose, smashing a blue hole in his head at the corner of his eye.

Yet Star wouldn't go down. The guns wavered in his hands, then as his knees slowly gave away, some reflex action brought the guns up. Both of them bellowed their defiance into the pouring rain, their flames stabbing, then winking out. As the echoes of the gunfire died, there was only the rain, pouring down into the crater like a great deluge.

Sherry rushed to him. "Oh, Ross! You're hurt! Did he hit you?"

He turned dazedly. He didn't feel hurt. "Get into that slicker!" he yelled above the roar of the rain. "We've got to pull out of here! Think of those rocks in this rain, and the lightning! Let's go!"

Fighting his way into his slicker, he saw the girl mount, and then he crawled into the saddle. The cattle moved when he started his horse toward them. Suddenly he made a resolution. He was taking them out—now.

Surprisingly the big steer that took the lead seemed to head into the cleft of his own choice, or possibly because it seemed to offer partial shelter from the sweep of the rain, or perhaps because he had seen so many of his fellows go that way in the weeks past.

Waving the girl ahead of him, Ross followed on into the cleft, casting scared glances aloft at the huge rocks. "Get on!" he yelled. "Get going!"

He glanced up again as they neared the narrowest part. He grabbed a stone and hurled it at a loitering steer, and the animal sprang ahead.

Sherry cast a frightened look upward and her eyes widened with horror. Her face went stark white as though she had been struck.

A thin trickle of stones fell, splashing into the cleft. A steer ahead stopped and bawled complainingly, and Ross grabbed a chunk of rock from the bank and hurled it, and the steer, hit hard, struggled madly to get ahead.

Sherry moved suddenly, closing up the gap between her horse and the nearest cattle, harrying them onward with stones and shouts. Ross looked up again, and, caught as in a trance, he saw the great slab stir ponderously, almost majestically. Its table-like top inclined, and then slowly, but with gathering impetus, it began to slide!

Shale and gravel rattled down the banks, and Ross touched spurs to his horse. The startled Appaloosa sprang ahead, forcing Flame into the steers, causing them to trot, and then, as the two horses crowded up into the folds of lava but out of the cleft in the crater wall, the air behind them was suddenly filled with a tremendous sound, a great, reverberating roar that seemed to last forever.

The rain forgotten, they sat, riveted in place, listening to the sound that was closing the crater forever, and leaving the body of Star Levitt as the only thing that would ever tell of human movement or habitation.

Yet as they remembered what Star Levitt had said about Berdue and Emmett Chubb, they unconsciously moved faster, and once out of the lava beds they left the cattle to shift for themselves and turned toward the mesa trail.

There was no let-up to the rain. It roared down in an increasing flood. They bowed their heads and hunched their slickers around them. The red of Flame's coat turned black with wet. Under his slicker, Ross rode with one hand on his gun, hoping for no trouble, but searching every clump of brush, every tree.

Rolly Burt ran from the cabin and grabbed their horses when they swung down. "Hustle inside an' get dry!" he yelled. "We've been worried as all get-out!"

When they got inside and had their slickers off, Mabry looked up, rolling a smoke. "Burt thought he saw Chubb today. We were worried about you."

"You haven't seen them?" Ross turned on him sharply.

Burt came in, overhearing the question. "No, an' I'm just as well satisfied. Say"—he looked up at them—"that danged geyser sure gives off some funny noises! I was over close when it sounded off the last time this afternoon, and I'd've swore I heard a human voice a-screechin'! That's one reason we have been worried about you two, although Bill did say you rode off the mesa."

Sherry's face blanched and she turned quickly toward an inner room.

Rolly stared after her. "Hey, what's the matter? Did I say something wrong?"

"No, just forget about it. And don't mention that geyser again." Then Ross explained, telling all that had happened during the long, wet afternoon, the end of Star Levitt, and the closing of the great cleft.

Sherry came out as they finished speaking. "Ross, those poor men. I hated them, but to think of anything human being caught in that awful place."

"Forget about it. They asked for it, and now it's all over. Look at that fire! It's our fire, in our own fireplace. Smell that coffee Mabry has on. And listen to the rain. That means the grass will be growin' tall an' green next year, honey, green on our hills an' for our cattle!"

She put a hand on his shoulder, and they stood there together, watching the flames dance, listening to the fire chuckling over the secrets locked in the wood, and hearing the great drops hiss out their anguish as they drowned themselves in the flames. A stick fell, and the blaze crept along it, feeling hungrily for good places to burn. From the kitchen they heard the rattle of dishes and the smell of bacon frying, and Rolly was pouring the coffee.

THE MAN FROM BATTLE FLAT

At half past four Krag Moran rode in from the
cañon trail, and within ten minutes half the town
knew that Ryerson's top gun hand was sitting in
front of the Palace.

Nobody needed to ask why he was there. It was
to be a showdown between Ryerson and the
Squaw Creek nesters, and the showdown was to
begin with Bush Leason.

The Squaw Creek matter had divided the
town, yet there was no division where Bush
Leason was concerned. The big nester had
brought his trouble on himself, and, if he got
what was coming to him, nobody would be
sorry. That he had killed five or six men was a
known fact.

Krag Moran was a lean, wide-shouldered
young man with smoky eyes and a still, Indian-
dark face. Some said he had been a Texas
Ranger, but all the town knew about him for sure
was that he had got back some of Ryerson's
horses that had been run off. How he would stack
up against a sure-thing killer like Bush Leason
was anybody's guess.

Bush Leason was sitting on a cot in his shack
when they brought him the news that Moran was
in town. Leason was a huge man, thick through
the waist and with a wide, flat, cruel face. When

they told him, he said nothing at all, just continued to clean his double-barreled shotgun. It was the gun that had killed Shorty Grimes.

Shorty Grimes had ridden for Tim Ryerson, and between them cattleman Ryerson and rancher Chet Lee had sewed up all the range on Battle Flat. Neither of them drifted cattle on Squaw Creek, but for four years they had been cutting hay from its grass-rich meadows, until the nesters had moved in.

Ryerson and Lee ordered them to leave. They replied the land was government land open to filing. Hedrow talked for the nesters, but it was Bush Leason who wanted to talk, and Bush was a troublemaker. Ryerson gave them a week and, when they didn't move, tore down fences and burned a barn or two.

In all of this Shorty Grimes and Krag Moran had no part. They had been repping on Carol Duchin's place at the time. Grimes had ridden into town alone and stopped at the Palace for a drink. Leason started trouble, but the other nesters stopped him. Then Leason turned at the door. "Ryerson gave us a week to leave the country. I'm giving you just thirty minutes to get out of town. Then I come a-shooting."

Shorty Grimes had been ready to leave, but after that he had decided to stay. A half hour later there was a challenging yell from the dark street out front. Grimes put down his glass and started for the door, gun in hand. He had just reached the street door when Bush Leason stepped through the back door and ran forward, three light, quick steps.

Bush Leason stopped then, still unseen. "Shorty," he called softly.

Pistol lowered, unsuspecting, Shorty Grimes had turned, and Bush Leason had emptied both barrels of the shotgun into his chest.

One of the first men into the saloon after the shooting was Dan Riggs, editor of *The Bradshaw Journal*. He knew what this meant, knew it and did not like it, for he was a man who hated violence and felt that no good could come of it. Nor had he any liking for Bush Leason. He had warned the nester leader, Hedrow, about him only a few days before.

Nobody liked the killing but everybody was afraid of Bush. They had all heard Bush make his brags and the way to win was to stay alive.

Now Dan Riggs heard that Krag Moran was in town, and he got up from his desk and took off his eye shade. It was no more than ninety feet from the front of the print shop to the Palace and Dan walked over. He stopped there in front of Krag. Dan was a slender, middle-aged man with thin hands and a quiet face. He said: "Don't do it, son. You mount up and ride home. If you kill Leason, that will just be the beginning."

"There's been a beginning. Leason started it."

"Now, look here . . . ," Riggs protested, but Krag interrupted him.

"You better move," he said in that slow Texas drawl of his. "Leason might show up any time."

"We've got a town here," Riggs replied determinedly. "We've got women and homes and decent folks. We don't want the town shot up and we don't want a lot of drunken killings. If you riders can't behave yourselves, stay away from town. Those farmers have a right to live, and they are good, God-fearing people."

Krag Moran just sat there. "I haven't killed anybody," he said reasonably, his face a little solemn. "I'm just a-sittin' here."

Riggs started to speak, then with a wave of exasperated hands he turned and hurried off. And then he saw Carol Duchin.

Carol Duchin was several things. By inheritance, from her father, she owned a ranch that would make two of Ryerson's. She was twenty-two years old, single, and she knew cattle as well as any man. Chet Lee had proposed to her three times and had been flatly refused three times. She both knew and liked Dan Riggs and his wife, and she often stopped overnight at the Riggs's home when in town. Despite that, she was cattle, all the way.

Dan Riggs went at once to Carol Duchin and spoke his piece. Right away she shook her head. "I won't interfere," she replied. "I knew Shorty Grimes and he was a good man."

"That he was," Riggs agreed sincerely, "I only wish they were all as good. That was a dastardly murder and I mean to say so in the next issue of my paper. But another killing won't help things any, no matter who gets killed."

Carol asked him: "Have you talked to Bush Leason?"

Riggs nodded. "He won't listen, either. I tried to get him to ride over to Flagg until things cooled off a little. He laughed at me."

She eyed him curiously.

"What do you want me to do?"

"Talk to Krag. For you, he'll leave."

"I scarcely know him." Carol Duchin was not planning to tell anyone how much she did know about Krag Moran, nor how interested in the tall rider she had become. During his period of repping with her roundup he had not spoken three words to her, but she had noticed him, watched him, and listened to her riders talk about him among themselves.

"Talk to him. He respects you. All of them do."

Yes, Carol reflected bitterly, *he probably does. And he probably never thinks of me as a woman.*

She should have known better. She was the sort of girl no man could ever think of in any other way. Her figure was superb, and she very narrowly escaped genuine beauty. Only her very coolness and her position as owner had kept more than one cowhand from speaking to her. So far only Chet Lee had found the courage. But Chet never lacked for that.

She walked across the street toward the Palace, her heart pounding, her mouth suddenly dry. Now that she was going to speak to Krag, face to face, she was suddenly frightened as a child. He got to his feet as she came up to him. She was tall for a girl, but he was still taller. His mouth was firm, his jaw strong and clean-boned. She met his eyes and found them smoky green and her heart fluttered.

"Krag"—her voice was natural at least—"don't stay here. You'll either be killed or you'll kill Bush. In either case it will be just one more step and will just lead to more killing."

His voice sounded amused, yet respectful, too. "You've been talking to Dan Riggs. He's an old woman."

"No"—suddenly she was sure of herself—"no, he's telling the truth, Krag. Those people have a right to that grass, and this isn't just a feud between you and Leason. It means good men are going to be killed, homes destroyed, crops ruined, and the work of months wiped out. You can't do this thing."

"You want me to quit?" He was incredulous. "You know this country. I couldn't live in it, nor anywhere the story traveled."

She looked straight into his eyes. "It often takes a braver man not to fight."

He thought about that, his smoky eyes growing somber. Then he nodded. "I never gave it any thought," he said seriously, "but I reckon you're right. Only I'm not that brave."

"Listen to Dan," she pleaded. "He's an intelligent man. He's an editor. His newspaper means something in this country and will mean more. What he says is important."

"Him?" Krag chuckled. "Why, ma'am, that little varmint's just a-fussin'. He don't mean nothing, and nobody pays much attention to him. He's just a little man with ink on his fingers."

"You don't understand," Carol protested.

Bush Leason was across the street. During the time Krag Moran had been seated in front of the Palace, Bush had been doing considerable serious thinking. How good Krag was, Bush had no idea, nor did he intend to find out; yet a showdown was coming, and from Krag's lack of action he evidently intended for Bush to force the issue.

Bush was not hesitant to begin it, but the more he considered the situation the less he liked it. The wall of the Palace was stone, so he could not shoot through it. There was no chance to approach Krag from right or left without being seen for some time before his shotgun would be within range. Krag had chosen his position well, and the only approach was from behind the building across the street.

This building was empty, and Bush had gotten inside and was lying there, watching the street when the girl came up. Instantly he perceived his advantage. As the girl left, Krag's eyes would involuntarily follow her. In that instant he would step from the door and shoot Krag down. It was simple and it was foolproof.

"You'd better go, ma'am," Krag said. "It ain't safe here. I'm staying right where I am until Leason shows."

She dropped her hands helplessly and turned away from him. In that instant, Bush Leason stepped from the door across the street and jerked his shotgun to his shoulder. As he did so, he yelled.

Carol Duchin was too close. Krag shoved her hard with his left hand and stepped quickly right, drawing as he stepped and firing as his right foot touched the walk.

Afterward, men who saw it said there had never been anything like it before. Leason whipped up his shotgun and yelled, and in the incredibly brief instant, as the butt settled against Leason's shoulder, Krag pushed the girl, stepped away from her, and drew. And he fired as his gun came level.

It was split-second timing and the fastest draw that anybody had ever seen in Bradshaw; the .45 slug slammed into Bush Leason's chest just as he squeezed off his shot, and the buckshot whapped through the air, only beginning to scatter at least a foot and a half over Krag Moran's head. And Krag stood there, flat-footed, and shot Bush again as he stood leaning back against the building. The big man turned sideways and fell into the dust off the edge of the walk.

As suddenly as that it was done. And then Carol Duchin got to her feet, her face and clothes dusty. She brushed her clothes with quick, impatient hands, and then turned sharply and looked at Krag Moran. "I never want to see you again!" she flared. "Don't put a foot on my place! Not for any reason whatever!"

Krag Moran looked after her helplessly, took an involuntary step after her, and then stopped. He glanced once at the body of Bush Leason and the men gathered around it. Then he walked to his horse. Dan Riggs was standing there, his face shadowed with worry. "You've played hell," he said.

"What about Grimes?"

"I know, I know. Bush was vicious. He deserved killing, and, if ever I saw murder, it was his killing of Grimes, but that doesn't change this. He had friends, and all of the nesters will be sore. They'll never let it alone."

"Then they'll be mighty foolish." Krag swung into the saddle, staring gloomily at Carol Duchin. "Why did she get mad?"

He headed out of town. He had no regrets about

the killing. Leason was a type of man that Krag had met before, and they kept on killing and making trouble until somebody shot too fast for them. Yet he found himself upset by the worries of Riggs as well as the attitude of Carol Duchin. Why was she so angry? What was the matter with everybody?

Moran had the usual dislike for nesters possessed by all cattlemen, yet Riggs had interposed an element of doubt, and he studied it as he rode back to the ranch. Maybe the nesters had an argument, at that. This idea was surprising to him, and he shied away from it.

As the days passed and the tension grew, he found himself more and more turning to thoughts of Carol. The memory of her face when she came across the street toward him and when she pleaded with him, and then her flashing and angry eyes when she got up out of the dust.

No use thinking about her, Moran decided. Even had she not been angry at him, what could a girl who owned the cattle she owned want with a drifting cowhand like himself? Yet he did think about her. He thought about her too much. And then the whole Bradshaw country exploded with a bang. Chet Lee's riders, with several hotheads from the Ryerson outfit, hit the nesters and hit them hard. They ran off several head of cattle, burned haystacks and two barns, killed one man, and shot up several houses. One child was cut by flying glass. And the following morning a special edition of *The Bradshaw Journal* appeared.

ARMED MURDERERS RAID
SLEEPING VALLEY

Blazing barns, ruined crops, and death remained behind last night after another vicious, criminal raid by the murderers, masquerading as cattlemen, who raided the peaceful, sleeping settlement on Squaw Creek.

Ephraim Hershman, 52 years old, was shot down in defense of his home by gunmen from the Chet Lee and Ryerson ranches when they raided Squaw Valley last night. Two other men were wounded, while young Billy Hedrow, 3 years old, was severely cut by flying glass when the night riders shot out the windows. . . .

Dan Riggs was angry and it showed all the way through the news and in the editorial adjoining. In a scathing attack he named names and bitterly assailed the ranchers for their tactics, demanding intervention by the territorial governor.

Ryerson came stamping out to the bunkhouse, his eyes hard and angry. "Come on!" he yelled. "We're going in and show that durned printer where he gets off. Come on! Mount up!"

Chet Lee was just arriving in town when the

cavalcade from the Ryerson place hit the outskirts of Bradshaw. It was broad daylight, but the
streets of the town were empty and deserted.

Chet Lee was thirty-five, tough as a boot, and
with skin like a sun-baked hide. His eyes were
cruel, his lips thin and ugly. He shoved Riggs
aside and his men went into the print shop,
wrecked the hand press, threw the type out into
the street, and smashed all the windows out of
the shop. Nobody made a move to harm Dan
Riggs, who stood pale and quiet at one side. He
said nothing to any of them until the end, and
then it was to Ryerson.

"What good do you think this will do?" he
asked quietly. "You can't stop people from
thinking. You can't throttle the truth. In the end it
always comes out. Grimes and Leason were shot
in fights, but that last night was wanton murder
and destruction of property."

"Oh, shut up!" Ryerson flared. "You're getting
off lucky."

Lee's little eyes brightened suddenly.
"Maybe," he said, "a rope is what this feller
needs!"

Dan Riggs looked at Lee without shifting an
inch. "It would be like you to think of that," he
said, and Lee struck him across the mouth.

Riggs got slowly to his feet, blood running
down his lips. "You're fools," he said quietly.
"You don't seem to realize that, if you can

destroy the property of others, they can destroy it for you. Or do you realize that when any freedom is destroyed for others, it is destroyed for you, too? You've wrecked my shop, ruined my press. Tyrants and bullies have always tried that sort of thing, especially when they are in the wrong."

Nobody said anything. Ryerson's face was white and stiff, and Krag felt suddenly uneasy. Riggs might be a fool but he had courage. It had been a rotten thing for Chet Lee to hit him when he couldn't fight back.

"We fought for the right of a free press and free speech back in 'Seventy-Six," Dan Riggs persisted. "Now you would try to destroy the free press because it prints the truth about you. I tell you now, you'll not succeed."

They left him standing there among the ruins of his printing shop and all he owned in the world, and then they walked to the Palace for a drink. Ryerson waved them to the bar.

"Drinks are on me!" he said. "Drink up!"

Krag Moran edged around the crowd and stopped at Ryerson's elbow. "Got my money, boss?" he asked quietly. "I've had enough."

Ryerson's eyes hardened. "What kind of talk is that?"

Chet Lee had turned his head and was staring hard at Moran. "Don't be a fool."

"I'm not a fool. I'm quitting. I want my money.

I'll have no part in that sort of thing this morning. It was a mean, low trick."

"You pointing any part of that remark at me?" Lee turned carefully, his flat, wicked eyes on Krag. "I want to know."

"I'm not hunting trouble." Krag spoke flatly. "I spoke my piece. You owe me forty bucks, Ryerson."

Ryerson dug his hand into his pocket and slapped two gold eagles on the bar. "That pays you off. Now get out of the country. I want no part of turncoats. If you're around here after twenty-four hours, I'll hunt you down like a dog."

Krag had turned away. Now he smiled faintly. "Why, sure. I reckon you would. Well, for your information, Ryerson, I'll be here."

Before they could reply, he strode from the room. Chet Lee stared after him. "I never had no use for that saddle tramp, anyway."

Ryerson bit the end off his cigar. His anger was cooling and he was disturbed. Krag was a solid man. Despite Lee, he knew that. Suddenly he was disturbed—or had it been ever since he saw Dan Riggs's white, strained face? Gloomily he stared down at his whiskey. What was wrong with him? Was he getting old? He glanced at the harsh face of Chet Lee—why wasn't he as sure of himself as Lee? Weren't they here first? Hadn't they cut hay in the valley for four years?

What right had the nesters to move in on them?

Krag Moran walked outside and shoved his hat back on his head. Slowly he built a smoke. Why, he was a damned fool! He had put himself right in the middle by quitting. Now he would be fair game for Leason's friends, with nobody to stand beside him. Well, that would not be new. He had stood alone before he came here, and he could again.

He looked down the street. Dan Riggs was squatted in the street, picking up his type. Slowly Krag drew on his cigarette, then he took it from his lips and snapped it into the gutter. Riggs looked up as his shadow fell across him. His face was still dark with bitterness.

Krag nodded at it. "Can you make that thing work again? The press, I mean."

Riggs stared at the wrecked machine. "I doubt it," he said quietly. "It was all I had, too. They think nothing of wrecking a man's life."

Krag squatted beside him and picked up a piece of the type and carefully wiped off the sand. "You made a mistake," he said quietly. "You should have had a gun on your desk."

"Would that have stopped them?"

"No."

"Then I'm glad I didn't have it. Although"—there was a flicker of ironic humor in his eyes—"sometimes I don't feel peaceful. There was a time this afternoon when if I'd had a gun. . . ."

Krag chuckled. "Yeah," he said, "I see what you mean. Now let's get this stuff picked up. If we can get that press started, we'll do a better job . . . and this time I'll be standing beside you."

Two days later the paper hit the street, and copies of it swiftly covered the country.

BIG RANCHERS WRECK
JOURNAL PRESS

Efforts of the big ranchers of the Squaw Creek Valley range to stifle the free press have proved futile. . . .

There followed the complete story of the wrecking of the press and the threats to Dan Riggs. Following that was a rehash of the two raids on the nesters, the accounts of the killings of Grimes and Leason, and the warning to the state at large that a full-scale cattle war was in the making unless steps were taken to prevent it.

Krag Moran walked across the street to the saloon, and the bartender shook his head at him. "You've played hob," he said. "They'll lynch both of you now."

"No, they wont. Make mine rye."

The bartender shook his head. "No deal. The boss says no selling to you or Riggs."

Krag Moran's smile was not pleasant. "Don't

make any mistakes, Pat," he said quietly. "Riggs might take that. I won't. You set that bottle out here on the bar or I'm going back after it. And don't reach for that shotgun. If you do, I'll part your hair with a bullet."

The bartender hesitated, and then reached carefully for the bottle. "It ain't me, Krag," he objected. "It's the boss."

"Then you tell the boss to tell me." Krag poured a drink, tossed it off, and walked from the saloon.

When Moran crossed the street, there was a sorrel mare tied in front of the shop. He glanced at the brand and felt his mouth go dry. He pushed open the door and saw her standing there in the half shadow—and Dan Riggs was gone.

"He needed coffee," Carol said quietly. "I told him I'd stay until you came back."

He looked at her and felt something moving deep within him, an old feeling that he had known only in the lonesome hours when he had found himself wanting someone, something— and this was it.

"I'm back." She still stood there. "But I don't want you to go."

She started to speak, and then they heard the rattle of hoofs in the street and suddenly he turned and watched the sweeping band of riders come up the street and stop before the shop. Chet Lee was there, and he had a rope.

Krag Moran glanced at Carol. "Better get out of here," he said. "This will be rough." And then he stepped outside.

They were surprised and looked it. Krag stood there with his thumbs hooked in his belt, his eyes running over them. "Hi," he said easily. "You boys figure on using that rope?"

"We figure on hanging an editor," Ryerson said harshly.

Krag's eyes rested on the old man for an instant. "Ryerson," he said evenly, "you keep out of this. I have an idea, if Chet wasn't egging you on, you'd not be in this. I've also an idea that all this trouble centers around one man, and that man is Chet Lee."

Lee sat his horse with his eyes studying Krag carefully. "And what of it?" he asked.

Riggs came back across the street. In his hand he held a borrowed rifle, and his very manner of holding it proved he knew nothing about handling it. As he stepped out in front of the cattlemen, Carol Duchin stepped from the print shop. "As long as you're picking on unarmed men and helpless children," she said clearly, "you might as well fight a woman, too."

Lee was shocked. "Carol! What are you doin' here? You're cattle!"

"That's right, Chet. I run some cows. I'm also a woman. I know what a home means to a woman. I know what it meant to Missus

234

Hershman to lose her husband. I'm standing beside Riggs and Moran in this . . . all the way."

"Carol!" Lee protested angrily. "Get out of there! This is man's work! I won't have it!"

"She does what she wants to, Chet," Krag said, "but you're going to fight me."

Chet Lee's eyes came back to Krag Moran. Suddenly he saw it there, plain as day. This man had done what he had failed to do; he had won. It all boiled down to Moran. If he was out of the way. . . .

"Boss"—it was one of Ryerson's men—"look out."

Ryerson turned his head. Three men from the nester outfit stood ranged at even spaces across the street. Two of them held shotguns, one a Spencer rifle. "There's six more of us on the roofs!" Hedrow called down. "Anytime you want to start your play, Krag, just open the ball."

Ryerson shifted in his saddle. He was suddenly sweating, and Krag Moran could see it. Nevertheless, Moran's attention centered itself on Chet Lee. The younger man's face showed his irritation and his rage at the futility of his position. Stopped by the presence of Carol, he was now trapped by the presence of the nesters.

"There'll be another day!" He was coldly furious. "This isn't the end!"

Krag Moran looked at him carefully. He knew all he needed to know about the man he faced.

Chet Lee was a man driven by a passion for power. Now it was the nesters, later it would be Ryerson, and then, unless she married him, Carol Duchin. He could not be one among many; he could not be one of two. He had to stand alone.

"You're mistaken, Chet," Moran said. "It ends here."

Chet Lee's eyes swung back to Krag. For the first time he seemed to see him clearly. A slow minute passed before he spoke. "So that's the way it is?" he said softly.

"That's the way it is. Right now you can offer your holdings to Ryerson. I know he has the money to buy them. Or you can sell out to Carol, if she's interested. But you sell out, Chet. You're the troublemaker here. With you gone, I think Ryerson and Hedrow could talk out a sensible deal."

"I'll talk," Hedrow said quietly, "and I'll listen."

Ryerson nodded. "That's good for me. And I'll buy, Chet. Name a price."

Chet Lee sat perfectly still. "So that's the way it is?" he repeated. "And if I don't figure to sell?"

"Then we take your gun and start you out of town," Krag said quietly.

Lee nodded. "Yeah, I see. You and Ryerson must have had this all figured out. A nice way to do me out of my ranch. And your quitting was all a fake."

236

"There was no plan," Moran said calmly. "You've heard what we have to say. Make your price. You've got ten minutes to close a deal or ride out without a dime."

Chet Lee's face did not alter its expression. "I see," he said. "But suppose something happens to you, Krag? Then what? Who here could make me toe the line? Or gamble I'd not come back?"

"Nothing's going to happen to me." Krag spoke quietly. "You see, Chet, I know your kind."

"Well"—Chet shrugged, glancing around—"I guess you've got me." He looked at Ryerson. "Fifty thousand?"

"There's not that much in town. I'll give you twelve, and that's just ten thousand more than you hit town with."

"Guess I've no choice," Chet said. "I'll take it." He looked at Krag. "All right if we go to the bank?"

"All right."

Chet swung his horse to the right, but, as he swung the horse, he suddenly slammed his right spur into the gelding's ribs. The bay sprang sharply left, smashing into Riggs and knocking him down. Only Krag's quick leap backwards against the print shop saved him from going down, too. As he slammed home his spur, Chet grabbed for his gun. It came up fast and he threw a quick shot that splashed Krag Moran's face

237

with splinters, then he swung his horse and shot, almost pointblank, into Krag's face.

But Moran was moving as the horse swung, and, as the horse swung left, Moran moved away. The second shot blasted past his face and then his own guns came up and he fired two quick shots. So close was Chet Lee that Krag heard the slap of the bullets as they thudded into his ribs below the heart.

Lee lost hold of his gun and slid from the saddle, and the horse, springing away, narrowly missed stepping on his face.

Krag Moran stood over him, looking down. Riggs was climbing shakily to his feet, and Chet was alive yet, staring at Krag.

"I told you I knew your kind, Chet," Krag said quietly. "You shouldn't have tried it."

Carol Duchin was in the café when Krag Moran crossed the street. He had two drinks under his belt and he was feeling them, which was rare for him. Yet he hadn't eaten and he could not remember when he had.

She looked up when he came through the door and smiled at him. "Come over and sit down," she said. "Where's Dan?"

Krag smiled with hard amusement. "Getting money from Ryerson to buy him a new printing outfit."

"Hedrow?"

"Him and the nesters signed a contract to supply Ryerson with hay. They'd have made a deal in the beginning if it hadn't been for Chet. Hedrow tried to talk business once before. I heard him."

"And you?"

He placed his hat carefully on the hook and sat down. He was suddenly tired. He ran his fingers through his crisp, dark hair. "Me?" He blinked his eyes and reached for the coffee pot. "I'm going to shave and take a bath. Then I'm going to sleep for twenty hours about, and then I'm going to throw the leather on my horse and hit the trail."

"I told you over there," Carol said quietly, "that I didn't want you to go."

"Uhn-uh. If I don't go now"—he looked at her somberly—"I'd never want to go again."

"Then don't go," she said.

And he didn't.

Center Point Publishing
600 Brooks Road ● PO Box 1
Thorndike ME 04986-0001 USA

(207) 568-3717

US & Canada:
1 800 929-9108
www.centerpointlargeprint.com